Inside Out
Book 3
of
The Undercity Series
by Kris Moger

This book is dedicated to my father because I miss him.

Chapter 1

C ate rushed ahead of Jolon. The hall was dark and smelly, the kind
of stench that made breathing difficult because the throat and
lungs protested the invasion of harmful chemicals. And the dark? Well,
the dark was worse.

"I never liked dark. I hated it before, but since our little trip into
sunshine, it just, well, it's darker. I feel like I'm going to dissolve into it
and never exist again."

Jolon's rambling wasn't what she wanted to listen to, but it was better than giving attention to the thoughts in her head. Long strands of
hair fell across her eye as she whipped her head about, trying to de-
termine where to go next. Frustrated, she swept the rogue locks back
and pulled her shirt close over her tank top, the chill of the air cutting through the thin fabric. Images of the outdoors kept invading her
brain, and she developed a new, aching yearning for freedom from
buildings.

Distracted, she led them forward at a brisk pace, though every tunnel looked the same and seemed to go nowhere.

"What was that?" she asked, realizing he was still talking.

"Perfect, love talking with you too. You realize I don't know anything about you except you're Caden's friend. Teddy thinks you're almost as interesting as a book, but me? I could easily have left you with
the cats."

"So charming. I could have easily left you in the kitchens."

"Hey, I didn't ask you to drag me along." He tugged at her coat. "Drop the pace a little, hey? My one leg keeps up fine, but this other one isn't so peppy."

She frowned at him but slowed. Sweat trickled down his broad nose while his round cheeks puffed in and out from heavy breathing. "Of all the people to get stuck with..."

"I end up with you," he finished for her, returning the disapproving scowl. "Yeah, neither of us likes this or each other, big surprise."

"Well, as long as we both agree, we'll do just fine." As she paused, she passed over the lantern. "Where are we?" she asked as she took out a length of string from her pocket and tied her curls of red hair back.

"Don't know," he said, glancing about, his copper complexion pallid.

"I thought you Petersons knew all about this place."

"Right. I've got the whole area all mapped out in my head. I'm one of those computer thingies Teddy's always babbling about. Pa's the one who explored this area: him and Teddy. I've never been here." He stopped in his tracks and slid down the wall, sitting with his knees drawn up close. "I just need a break. There's a fist in my chest, and it's making a squishy toy out of my heart," he said, his voice just above a whisper.

The lantern clanged on the cement as he dropped the light aside before burying his head in his arms.

"Tired."

"Ah, you're always tired," she said with a little compassion. She dropped down beside him and huddled close. "Cold in here. We need to find some place better soon."

Jolon sniffed and glanced down both sides of the narrow, empty hall. "Don't think anyone's following us. Maybe we could go back and sneak a peek, see if everything's settled down?"

She shook her head. "Not likely. Those Uppers who showed up are a devil lot, and I think they've taken over your tower world."

"Then we should go back and help."

"How?"

Open-mouthed, he stared as though hoping a brilliant idea would tumble out, but nothing came. "Hate this," he muttered and clenched his jaw shut.

Sore and adrift, she gave him an awkward pat on the arm. "I'm sure everyone is okay. At least, I think so."

"You're terrible at this comforting stuff, you realize that, right?"

"Pththt," she replied, sticking out her tongue. "I'm doing my best. What where those things they had?"

He snatched up a pebble and tossed it against the wall across from them. The stone clacked and clattered as it bounced, the sound echoing down the corridor. "Pa says they're called guns. We always had to keep an eye out for them."

"Find any?"

"Once. Didn't get to keep it or try it out. Pa took it and threw it in the southern pit. He said if our world ever got a hold of guns, life would get much more deadly."

"Too bad he wasn't the only one who thought getting rid of them was a good idea."

"What are you doing here, Jolon?"

Startled, they scrambled to their feet. Cate snatched up the lantern and held it in front of her ready to use it as a weapon if she had to.

The woman standing before them was older than Caden's parents, but well groomed with several braids of grey hair wrapped around her head, a rusty, freckled complexion, and eyes the colour of polished wood. She was relatively thick and wore several layers of shirts over a heavy floral skirt.

"It's okay." Jolon placed a hand on her arm. "It's Nuna, the one who found the tower first."

With a hesitant step, he hugged her, his expression revealing his relief.

"Woah, well, what's this? What's going on, boy?" she asked, pushing him away to see his face. "You and your girlfriend get lost?"

Cate put up her hands, the light flickering around them as it swung. "Oh, wait. He's not, I'm not...."

"No, we're not anything or lost. Well, yeah, sort of... lost that is. Not the other thing. Teddy's the one... ugh," he grunted as Cate caught him with her elbow.

Nuna chuckled and beckoned them to follow. "Come on. Let's get you back to where you belong. It's cold down here if you don't dress in layers."

"No, we can't go back," both he and Cate said.

"Huh? Why?"

Cate exchanged a glance with Jolon, unsure of where to start.

Sighing, Nuna wrapped an arm around Jolon. "Come on, back to my place. First, we'll warm you both up and sort out what's what after that."

"Don't you need a light?" Cate asked as they traveled down the gloomy passage.

"Nope. Not in these parts," she said with a touch of pride. "Know them too well. Besides, I got electric lights running just a couple of turns from here."

Jolon shuddered and kept beside her, taking comfort in the older woman's presence.

Cate dropped back behind them, overwhelmed by recalled impressions of the attack of the Upperlords. Every step they took reverberated through the passageway like the horrible explosion from Belinda's gun, making her breath catch in her chest. The screams, chaos, and memory of Jolon's father falling to the ground—she wanted to forget, but couldn't.

People, why did she ever get involved with people? They were unreasonable and untrustworthy and had issues she didn't understand.

"Henri, Henri? " Teddy called, shaking the brute's forearm. The room was dim, and the cold of the refuse-covered cement floor chilled him through to the marrow. He pushed back Henri's dark hair matted with blood and checked to see if the bleeding had stopped.

The man grunted and opened his eyes, which took a moment to focus on Teddy's face.

"Where we?" the brute asked as he struggled to a seated position.

"Ah, I'm not certain." Teddy sat back and winced as the movement aggravated his ankle.

"Hurt lots?"

He grasped his leg, his jaw tight against the pain. "Oh, yeah, just a little more than I'd like." Dirt clung to his sweaty brown hair—a remnant picked up from sleeping on the floor amid the garbage.

Henri served him a cursory once over. "You so skinny boy. How you enough muscle to move?"

"I'm wiry," Teddy said, coughing as dust crawled down his throat. Water would be helpful. "You okay? That was quite a blow you took."

"What? Oh, right," he said as he put a hand to his head and grimaced. "I remember. Big guy clocked me from behind. Not fair fighting."

"Yeah, you went down pretty hard. This is all such a mess." An overwhelming flood of emotions created moisture that welled up in his eyes. "I don't know where anyone is or if they're all okay. Pa, oh, Pa..."

"He all right?"

Tears rolled down Teddy's face as he shook his head. With a snuffling grunt, he rubbed at his cheeks, his shirt stinking of musty garbage and oil. "I don't know. Belinda's creepers dragged him away. I tried to get to him, but that weasel Dorkas cut me off."

"Caden? Deb and Ma? What about them? Jolon?" asked Henri, his tawny-grey skin flushing up his neck as his jade eyes tightened.

Teddy stared at the rubbish-filled space in front of him, shaking. "I don't know. Wish I did, but...." he tossed his hands up, "I don't have a clue." Careful of his foot, he worked his way up the wall, trying to stand. The brick was slick with a molding slime and the place stunk much like a sewer. A slit of light filtered in through a tiny opening in the door.

Henri forced himself to his feet too. The brute staggered over, peering through the crack.

"Looks like some store. Back of store, I think. Shelves and stuff out there. Light coming from..." he craned his neck, trying to get a better view, "can't tell."

Weakness coursed through Teddy's muscles, and he leaned against the wall, limp like an empty ragged shirt. "I don't know what to do. I've run out of ideas. Pa...." A horrible ache settled on him.

Henri stepped toward him his broad face marred with confused helplessness. The brute clenched his fists and turned back to the exit, anger burning through his face. With a tremendous roar, he smashed at the door. The wood wobbled and shook on the hinges.

"Stop that!" someone yelled from the other side, but he didn't bother trying to see who it was. The guard shoved the point of a weapon in the little window. "You don't stop, and I'll use this. Put some holes in that thick head of yours."

Whatever effect the guard was hoping for, he didn't get. Henri bellowed and smashed until the door buckled and collapsed, crashing onto the person on the other side. The guy tried to get up, but Henri tromped on the door and kicked the other brute in the head.

"And stay down," he yelled as the guy's head lolled sideways.

Henri turned back toward Teddy and threw him over his shoulder.

"Uh, Henri?" Teddy grunted as he wriggled about. Ugly mauve tiling and empty metal shelves flitted by, making him dizzy. "How about putting me down?"

"No."

"Henri, this is not comfortable flopping about on your back. Honest, you can put me down."

"Nope. You broken. Must move quick."

Teddy shifted on the brute's shoulder. "Well, at least, tell me where we are. What do you see?"

He paused by the entrance, Teddy dangling down his back with a better view of Henri's backside than he wanted. "Nothing. Never been to this area. Different. No one around. People all gone."

"Must be the tunnel they used to find us. This area seems to be a maze of shops all connecting to each other. Umm, You need to put me down, Henri. I'm getting a headache and seeing spots."

Grabbing him by the waistband, Henri twisted around and lowered him to the floor. He staggered and kept a grip on the brute's arm, his face hot with blood.

"Oh, that's better. Now I just need to stop the ringing in my head."

"Find others. Which way we go? Where others? Why you and me separate?"

Ears ringing, Teddy pressed the heels of his hands against his thumping temples and tried to decide which way to go. The hall dissolved to darkness in both directions.

"Good questions, all of them. Wish I had answers, but I don't understand what Belinda and her cohorts are up to either. Here, give me an arm and let's go this way." He pointed to the left. "Seems a little brighter."

Wary of being heard, they crept along the wall with Henri supporting him. They passed several ransacked shops with little left in them, but broken shelves and piles of trash. Henri picked up a stout leg of a table and handed it to him to use as a support. The sound of murmuring voices echoed down to them, and they slowed, inching along carefully so as not to get caught.

Henri pulled out a gun and gripped it the same way Belinda had.

Teddy grabbed his sleeve, his eyes wide. "What? Where did you get that?"

He gestured back the way they came. "The guard."

"A gun. You don't even know how to use a gun, do you?"

Henri stared at it, the weapon awkward in his meaty hand. "Simple enough. One end to hold, the other end to spit out the little piece of metal that make holes in people, and the bit of a trigger makes metal fly." He shrugged. "Point and pull?"

Exasperated, Teddy pushed his hair back from his face and scowled. "Point and pull, I guess. Just be careful where you point. Those things are dangerous, and we don't want to put holes in anyone if we don't need to."

"No, no holes. Just scare," Henri assured him. He went to put the weapon away, but Teddy stopped him.

"Better leave it out until we find out who's up ahead. If it's Dorkas, I might not object to you putting a hole in him somewhere. Not anywhere that would kill him; just make him leak a little."

Cate sat down at Nuna's kitchen table. The woman put a plate of stew in front of her, but she wasn't hungry. Instead of eating, she stirred the mess and pushed a hunk of potato about with a fork. Jolon sat across from her and didn't seem to be able to eat either. Nuna's golden dog put its wedge head on his lap and stared up at him. He petted the animal, offering the hound a tidbit of meat.

"Well, that's quite the turn of events," Nuna said after they explained what happened. She leaned back in her chair and put her feet up on a box. "So, Georges was right in the end. Those Upperlords found you and asserted their authority." Her worn features twisted with disgust.

"Authority. Right. Ownership and domination. Despise the type."

"Yeah, well, thing is, now what do we do?" Jolon asked.

Cate stared at her plate—fork abandoned—and struggled with a nagging desire to help and the well-practiced habit of keeping her distance.

Nuna shrugged. "Guess you need to find another place to live. I doubt they'll spread this far."

"So, what? You don't have to move? You can stay here and hide while everyone else..."

"Oh, don't start that again," she snapped, cutting Jolon off, her aged, ruddy face flushing and thin lips tightening. "I helped out the last time, remember? I let all of you come here, and I didn't get too much out of it. Okay, yes, I got company, but some of that company wasn't so wonderful, and I'm not about to risk what little life left me to sort out any Upper problems."

Caden's brother stared at her, his disappointment clear.

"Perfect. What about you? Cate? We need to find the others."

Aggravated, she snatched up the fork and stabbed a piece of carrot. The last thing she wanted was to get within fifty feet of Uppercity. Uppers were poison, a corrosive acid eating away anything good. "No, actually, we don't. At least, I don't. What? Don't look so shocked. I told you all before I'm not interested in happy little utopias. I've got plans of my own, and they don't include rescuing a bunch of idealistic dreamers. There's a whole world outside with enough space for everyone. Why would I bother fighting over this dugout hole?"

"That's just terrific," Jolon snapped, sending his plate and contents flying as he leaped to his feet. "You are...."

"What? Wait," Nuna cut in.

"Yeah, I'm what?" Cate demanded, getting up and jamming her fists against the table. "Go on, what am I?"

"What are you talking about, outside," Nuna demanded, rising too. The dog started barking. "Quiet, Toro."

"You're a selfish..."

"All right, that's enough," shouted Nuna, grabbing them both by the arm. "What do you mean, outside? No one can go outside."

Jolon pulled back, his stance defiant. The woman's face was a mix of terror and hope. "Yes, we can, and we have."

Cate returned the glare he tossed her but pulled her hair out of its tie, so the tresses fell across her eye. "Yeah, outside where Uppers don't exist, and stuff can grow. That's where I'm going and if you've got a problem with that, too bad."

"Go, if that's the way you feel. Ah, don't you care about Teddy, or Deb, or even Caden? Fine. You make a lousy friend, anyway. That's what I told them, but they didn't agree. Well, ha, ha. I win. You're not worth their love and affection, so who needs you." He glared at Nuna. "Either of you. I don't. I'll go find 'em myself."

"Just hold on, boy," Nuna said, grasping his arm. "Back up. You honestly went outside? Outside; as in out in the trees and the sunshine? Without protection?"

"Yes, gah, yes! Who cares? It doesn't matter," he shouted, wrenching his arm away.

"Oh, calm down, dopy," Cate said, sitting back down. She gave him her best dirty scowl. "Fine. I'll give you a hand for a moment, but when we get the others out of here I'm done. Got that?"

"Ah, don't do me any favors."

Anger soared through Cate as she twisted her arms over her chest and tightened her jaw in defiance. "Don't worry, I'm not. I just can't stand the thought of you stumbling about trying to be all hero-like. It was bad enough enduring Teddy's adventure into bravery. I don't need to be ghosted by you and your bad decisions."

They jumped as Nuna slammed a fist on the table.

"You went outside," she shouted, flicking her hair back as it fell out of its bun. "You silly children. Don't you realize what you're saying?"

"What? What are we saying?" Jolon asked, staring at her. "How is going outside going to help us?"

He sat down, his words sinking in. "Oh, we could go outside and go around to Uppercity. We could show everyone they don't need the tower, that we could leave and spread out, find space for everyone."

Cate laughed. "You think they'll care?"

"Do you have any better ideas?"

Nuna tossed carrots at both of them. "Would you two stop bickering? Gah, I'm going to have to go along just to keep you from killing each other."

Jolon shoved his chair aside and stomped to the door. "Honestly, I don't care what you two do. I'm going to find a way out of here and find the others."

He stormed out, absconding a lantern as he went. Toro trailed behind, snuffing at his heels.

Cate sat for a moment until the guilt got to her. All she could picture was Caden and Deb stuck in some Upper hole, and Teddy, well, she tried not to picture him at all.

"Ahgh," she said and slung her pack across her body. She snatched up Jolon's stash and followed Nuna out the door.

They caught up with Jolon at a crossroad where he held his light high, trying to decide which way to go.

"Left," Nuna said behind him. "You want to go left. It leads up." She strode past and patted her pup on the head. He yipped and scampered along.

Cate thrust his stash in his gut. "Here. You're gonna need this stuff, and I'm not gonna carry everything. Let's go, hero. We'll think of a better plan as we go."

With a glare, he grunted at her and slung his stash on his back. "Fine. The sooner we get this over with the better."

"Bunch a fools," someone laughed as Teddy and Henri peered around the corner. "They thought they could keep all this to themselves."

"Yeah," said the one Teddy recognized as Dorkas. The creeper's words slurred as though he had been drinking. "Ah, they never got the way of things. Them Petersons always thought themselves as better than Uppers. Ya know, their warehouse? That was my grandpa's way back. He was the one who found it. Not Peterson's ragged, thieving grandpa's." He belched and slammed a bottle on a table. "They stole it, took it. It was mine. My inheritance. Not theirs. But I got them back, now. I got 'em and they ain't gonna think themselves so special now."

"Yep, you got 'em," laughed his companion. They clinked bottles and toasted each other.

Teddy tugged on Henri's sleeve. The brute put the gun in his pocket as they leaned back out of sight and crept back into a shadow-filled alcove.

"So, that's why Dorkas always slinked about the warehouse as though it was his. Always hated that man."

"It true? Your pa take from his pa?"

"No. At least, I don't think so." Teddy thought back over all his father's stories. "My pa would have said something about that if it were true. Pa is a good man, and his pa was too. Dorkas is a creeper who comes from a slug family."

"That may be your opinion, little rat, but in my books, it's the other way around."

Henri jumped to his feet, shielding Teddy. Dorkas split a hideous grin across his face while his companion pointed a gun at them.

"Ah, don't you even try, lump. You ain't no real brute an' we'll spill you before you can blink," Dorkas said, wavering on his feet.

Teddy yelped in pain as the creeper kicked at his injured foot.

Henri lunged forward, but Teddy seized his leg, pulling him back.

"No, no wait," he gasped, hauling himself up. "Don't, Henri, they've got us."

"Yeah, that's right," Dorkas' buddy crowed. "We've got ya, and we're gonna toss you right back in the trash."

"Where's my family, my pa and ma, and the others," Teddy demanded, gripping Henri's arm for support.

He leaned in close, his breath a disgusting stench of rotting teeth and booze. "Wouldn't you like to know."

Dorkas smacked the guy on the arm. "Eh, back off, Creb. Might as well put them with the others. Keep all the scum together. They'll be all parceled off soon enough." He motioned for them to go forward. "Come on, let's get going."

Creb chuckled and kept his gun pointed at them, so there was no opportunity to escape. "Gonna be all separated," he chortled, thrusting his dirt-crusted, oily, pasty face close. "Gonna sell you off."

He yelped as Dorkas smacked him in the back of the head. "Shut it. They'll find out soon enough what their fate is."

The Creb creeper fell in behind as Dorkas led them. Henri put an arm around Teddy, supporting him as they went down the passage.

"Why you stop me?" Henri whispered, his hatred for the scum so intense his eyes burned like they could almost put holes in the back of Dorkas' stringy-haired head.

Teddy clutched his arm; his breathing labored from the pain moving caused his foot. "Several reasons, we were at a disadvantage, they had a gun on us, I don't want to lose you, and I want to find out where the others are."

Henri grunted. "Guess makes sense. Still don't like, though. Want to smash face."

"You'll get your chance. Just keep your gun hidden," Teddy whispered before saying aloud, "Where are we going? To Uppercity?"

"Ah, you are not as stupid as your pa, are you?" Dorkas sneered. "Yep. Auction house is all set up and ready. Gonna sell you all off. You might be damaged goods at the moment, but as soon as you're all healed," he paused and chuckled, "Yep. They expect to get a good price for you."

"You scum. Worse than scum. You what scum calls scum," Henri said, his hand grasping the gun in his pocket.

Teddy put his hand over Henri's. "No. It's all good."

"Yeah, keep your lump in check. Ain't got no patience for his babbling," Crub said, pushing at Henri's back with his gun.

Chapter 2

"You sure this is safe?" Nuna asked as they stood in front of a grey metal door.

"Depends on your idea of safe," Cate said, skirting around her and pushing on the handle. Sunlight flooded in, and Nuna yelped, putting her arms in front of her face.

Jolon put a hand on her shoulder as the wind blew in with fresh air. "Don't listen to her. It is safe. Come on."

Cate stepped outside, and Jolon followed while Nuna inched her way through the doorway. Tears made her pale eyes sparkle. "This is incredible. All this time, all this time," she whispered, her head shaking. "We could have opened a door and went outside, and she would still be with me."

Whoever the woman was talking about, Cate didn't have any idea, but she suspected that Jolon did as he put a sympathetic hand on her shoulder.

"Everybody thought venturing outside wasn't safe," he told her, kicking at a lump of grass. "Nobody realized it was okay to go out. We wouldn't have known if Deb hadn't wandered away."

"I knew," Cate said, standing by the wall. "One of the cats from the bookstore went out. I figured if the animal could survive, so could I."

"Thanks for sharing," Jolon said as though she had done something wrong.

"Hey, I was gonna say; I was waiting till I was sure I was okay."

"And when was that? Before or after we all died?"

"Okay, you two. That's enough." Nuna stepped between them. She glanced toward the sun as though it was going to attack her. "Where do we go from here?"

They stood at the base of a hill covered in long grass and flowers, with the mall and the tower behind them, obstructing the sightline of Uppercity. Jolon scrambled up the hill, and they came up behind him.

"Everything is so different from the outside," he said, scanning the area. He pointed to the left then the right. "Is Upper that way or that way?"

Cate put her hands to her hips and pulled her lower lip in with her teeth. He was right. They had no markers to go by. "Good question. Here's another. Is going to Uppercity our best course of action? Is that where everyone will be or did those Uppers stuff them somewhere else?"

"True," Nuna said. She bent down and ran her hands over the grass as though she wanted to be sure the vegetation was real. "At this point, we're guessing, aren't we?"

"So, are you saying we should give up?" Jolon asked, exasperated with both of them.

"No," she replied and sat down, her hairy legs sticking out in front of her from under her skirt. "I'm not certain what to do."

"Oh, this is perfect," said Jolon, tossing his hands up. He laced his fingers behind his head and groaned. "Fine bunch of rescuers we are. Can't even pick a direction. Where the hell is Teddy when I need him."

"Hey. Forget the old guy. We can do this," Cate said, his words hitting a nerve. "All we need to do is decide on a direction, right? Well, when we got lost before, we found those greenhouse buildings and made our way from there, right?"

"Yeah, but that was on the other side of the building."

She stuck her thumb at him. "Exactly. Simple as it seems, I think all we need to do is go in the opposite direction."

"I'm gonna ignore your annoying sarcasm, and assume you're right. When we went back, we traveled to the left. So, if we want to go back, we should travel to the right. Great, let's go." He went back down the hill and kept on going, keeping the building on his right.

"And do what when we get there?" Cate asked, coming behind him. "Walk up to the glass and knock? I'm sure they'll just let us in. They loved what you guys found before; they should adore expanding their world so much they don't count anymore."

"What are you talking about?" he asked, working his way along the uneven ground.

"Those Uppers, they aren't going to be happy if people can spread out and fend for themselves. Picture it, all the little gardens with all their private homes, people hunting and growing stuff, and everything. Everyone with a miniature Upper world all their own. They'll just love that."

Jolon threw her a dirty look. "I don't care. I'm tired of hearing about how unhappy the Uppers are gonna be about every little thing everyone else does. They took my family. They've got 'em, and they hurt 'em. I can't say if Pa's okay, or even still alive. I do know what they want to do with Teddy. You know what they want to do with Teddy?"

Cate clamped her lips shut, refusing to dwell on what he was implying.

He stepped in close, getting right next to her. "I bet you can guess. And that's what they want to do with Deb too, isn't that a wonderful thought."

The old, familiar dread crept up her spine and twisted knots in her stomach along the way. Images of his little sister standing at the auction dock while people leered at her as though she was an object made for their amusement made her swallow acidic bile. "Fine, I get your point. Let's get the sewer scum," she said, stepping around him.

Jolon uttered a dark chuckle. "Sure, now you're all fired, up. That was a quick switch you flipped."

She spat on the ground and tromped on ahead of him. "Don't question my loyalty, all right? I might be somewhat selfish, but I'm not gonna let them do anything to that little girl. I know what they are like. I've been there."

"Haven't we all in one way or another," Jolon murmured as though remembering his childhood.

Ignoring him, she glanced back at Nuna, who was trailing behind, stopping to touch a flower here and a leaf there. Cate groaned and ran her hands through her hair. What was she going to do? She had one dreamer distracted by every little leaf that blew her way, and her other companion was an anxious, sarcastic pessimist who was good at smart remarks and not much else, as far as she figured. Yes, they were the perfect team to march in and rescue the world.

Toro trotted up and licked her fingers, his happy dog-face optimistic. She sighed and scratched behind his ears, hoping someone better would come along and save them.

After several hours, their trail cut through a square cement area with curved benches and an iron statue. Vines crawled all over the figure obscuring the exact form of the sculpture.

Nuna brushed away some plants from one of the benches and sunk onto the cement seat. "How much further do you think we have to go?"

"Depends on where we're trying to get to. If we want another way into Upper, we shouldn't need to go as far as the greenhouses." She paused and took a bar from her bag, tearing open the package and taking a bite. "All we need to do is find an entrance that isn't barred and slip in. That should be easy. Uppers are such trusting souls."

"Sarcasm is not helpful." Nuna said, digging through her stash for something to eat.

"No, but she has a point," Jolon said, and she twitched, uncomfortable with the thought that he almost agreed with her. "I don't know much about Uppercity. I don't know the layout or what doors open to where. The best I can think is that the greenhouses seem like the weak spot. I know the windows are not only sealed, but also made of un-breakable glass and so are the doors, but we could sneak in. We could break a lock or something and get in that way."

"And we're back to my original question. How far do we need to go?"

Jolon pursed his lips and picked up a tiny purple flower. He twirled it between his fingers. "Good question. I wish I knew."

"Perfect," Nuna said, slapping her hands on her lap. "Well, if we don't know where we're going, we might as well try and get there as soon as possible."

Caden sat between Ma and Deb, holding both of them close. Every piece of her body twitched with pain. They huddled on a low couch in a narrow room with bamboo furniture and several broad windows. Georges sat across from them, floral suit torn and bloody and tight braids askew. Her midnight black skin dripped with sweat while her boney hands shook as she clenched and unclenched them on her lap.

"Ma?" Caden brushed her mother's frizzy blond hair from her ashen face. "Ma, I'm sure he's fine. I'm sure everyone's fine."

Her mother whimpered and snuffled, her pale blue eyes bloodshot and her narrow nose red. "Deb, my little Deb."

Caden kissed her head. "She's asleep, Ma. She's cried herself to sleep."

"I'm so sorry, Tisha," Georges whispered, her voice broken into pieces. "I don't understand how this happened." She tossed a hand about. "No, I do. I understand every little piece of evil that makes up my sister's selfish body and soul. I should have realized she would worm a way into the tower." With a twisted, pathetic laugh, she dragged shaking fingers over her face. "I did realize it. I sensed in the bottom of my being she would show up, but I hid in a lie, pretending we were safe. Oblivion came back to bite me in the backside."

"Where did they get the guns?" Caden asked, wishing she had one of her own.

Georges' thick lips twisted in disgust as she shook her head. "Didn't even suspect they had weapons like that. And bullets, they have bullets. Can't believe it."

"You're not helping," Caden growled as Ma buried her face in her hands. "Ma."

She lifted her head and pushed her hair back. "I'll be all right. I'll be fine." She hiccupped. "I just need a moment."

Deb squirmed about, shoving her legs against the arm of the couch. The white bamboo weave cracked at the pressure of her worn runners catching on the wood.

Ma ran her fingers through Deb's hair. "Let's let her stretch out. She's best off sleeping."

Caden slipped out from under her sister and laid Deb's head on a pale pink cushion. She worked the kinks out of her limbs, straightening with care as sharp pangs made her cringe. Rolling her neck, she moved aside while her mother spread a knitted blanket over Deb.

Georges curled up tight into her chair and chewed on a fingernail. "I need a drink, a long, hard, gut-eating drink."

"Yeah, that would help everything," Caden said, wandering to one of the windows.

"It would help me."

"Forget about your drink. Where are we, Georges? You must have some idea."

The other woman dissolved into a defeated half-shrug. "Eh, some-where, I guess."

Ma stood in front of her, brows drawn together so tight she had the appearance of a snake about to strike. "That's it? That's all you can say... somewhere? And what good is that to us?"

"I'm sorry, I don't know what to tell you. I'm..." she slumped down further, her head falling to the side, "so tired."

Ma glanced at Caden, her anger turning to worry. "Georges?"

The Upperlord waved a limp few fingers as though that was all she could summon. "I'm fine. Just weary. Arm hurts, neck, chest, jaw hurts. Pulled a muscle or something."

Kneeling in front of the older woman, Ma grabbed her wrist and checked her pulse. Her frown deepened. "Caden, check for some water in that jug over by the door."

The ceramic jug was full, and there were a couple of orange plastic glasses beside it. She filled one and brought it to her mother. "At least, they don't want us to die of thirst."

"How thoughtful of them," her mother said and held up the cup to Belinda's lips. The other woman scowled and tried to pull away.

"Yuck. What is that stuff?"

Ma sniffed the liquid and took a sip. "Water. Take some."

"Eh, you're mean," Georges said but did as ordered.

"She okay, Ma?" Caden asked, standing by them.

Her mother got back up, her lips tight with concern. "I'm not sure. Her eyes are unfocused, and she's sweating profusely. She might have the flu, but the pain in her chest might be something more."

"What can we do?"

Ma cast her gaze about the room. "There's not much here. Check those cupboards over there. Maybe there's something in them to help, a blanket or a pillow. Georges should lie down, and we'll prop her feet up."

Caden went to the low row of fake wood cupboards and pulled on the brass handles. "They're locked, Ma. Sorry."

"Figures," she said as she threw some cushions on the beige carpet. "We'll make due with what we have. Help me get her on the floor."

"What you doing?" Georges asked as Caden took hold of her arm. "Don't want to move."

"Come on, dear," Ma said, coaxing her out of the chair. They helped the Upperlord lie down on her side, and Ma propped her feet up so that they were slightly higher than her head. After, she pulled off her sweater and spread it over the other woman's shoulders.

The door opened, and Caden whirled around. An ancient, wrinkled blob of a woman stood there with a tray in her hands and a sneer on her cracked face.

"Ehgh, junk on floor again, hey." She tossed out a mean chuckle and stuck the tray on the counter. "Jes give her a hit a something, and she'll perk right up," she said as she hobbled out of the room.

Two brutes hung out on the other side of the entrance. So much for trying to get out.

Deb rubbed her eyes and yawned as she sat up. "I smell food."

"Yeah, there's some soup and biscuits over there on that tray." Caden pointed to the food. "Hey, Ma, you should eat some too."

"Mmmh," her mother said, her attention focused on Georges.

"She doing better?" she asked, kneeling beside Ma. The Upperlord was pasty and limp, her breath shallow.

"She's weak, but her heart is beating more steady. It was running faster than a rat escaping from the catchers." Ma stood, arcing her back as she did so. Her vertebra cracked, and she massaged her neck.

Caden offered her a bowl of soup. "Mushroom, I think. Smells like it."

Her mother took the food with a half-smile. "Thank you. At least, they are willing to feed us. We must take that as a good sign."

"Must we?" Caden poked a spoon in her bowl. Dejected, she sat down beside Deb and forced herself to eat. "I don't think I can take anything they do as a good sign."

"What are they going to do with us, Ma?" Deb whispered, her pale eyes afraid. "I want to go home."

Caden hugged her, and Ma sat on the other side of them. "Don't worry, dearest. We'll work our way out of this."

"Where do you think the others are?" Caden asked just as the door opened again.

"Aw, are you missing your pathetic family?" drawled Dorkas, his greasy face smug. "Don't be so sad, we've brought you a couple of friends."

He moved aside, and the brutes behind him pushed Teddy and Henri into the room.

"Teddy!" Ma rushed over to him, wrapping him in her arms. "Oh, my boy, are you all right?"

"Yeah," he said, his voice muffled by Ma's embrace. She helped him over to Georges' vacated chair; his face was tight with pain. "Leg hurts. That's all."

Henri stood behind him. "He good."

"Yeah, he good, you good, all good, aren't you, miserable thieves," Dorkas sneered and loomed over Ma as she bent to check Teddy's foot. "You got what you all deserved, didn't you?"

With pinpoint eyes of hate and a low-chest growl, Henri stepped between them.

"Oh, ho. So what you gonna do, lump?" He waved a hand at his fellow creepers gathered by the door. "You gonna attack me and risk their lives? You're a nothing, just like them."

"Henri, wait," Caden said, taking his hand. She stood by Teddy and Ma and motioned for Deb to get behind them. "You're right, Dorkas," she said, facing him. "We're not going to do anything. You possess everything now, so why don't you just let us go."

The creeper snickered and paced before them. "Let you go? Just like that? To do what? To live where?" He jabbed himself in the chest, his hairy chin sticking out. "I got your home now, your warehouse, your towers, your everything."

"No, you don't." Teddy tried to get to his feet.

Henri pushed him back down. "Sit."

"I'm not a puppy," he replied irritably but stayed seated. "You don't have anything. Belinda does. And all the other Upperlords do. Do you think they are going to share anything with you? Ha, they might let you keep the warehouse, but that's about all. Then again, there's not much left, is there?"

"Ah, shut your hole," the creeper said with a raised hand ready to strike, but Henri towered over him. "Eh, you lot aren't worth the bother. Not anymore." He tried to take on a bored countenance, but he backed away, fear in his eyes.

"Where's Truman?" Ma asked, getting to her feet. Tears streaked her face as she reached out to him. "Where's my husband?"

The creeper shrugged as though she was inquiring about a bug. "Don't know. Bottom of a hole, probably. That's what ya do with the garbage."

Caden didn't even see Henri move, but she did see Dorkas fly back into his cohorts. Screeching, he put a hand up to his eye. "You'll regret that! I'll make sure you pay for that." He stumbled out the door with the others close behind.

"That wasn't the best idea," Teddy said, leaning back in his chair. "Great fun to witness, though."

The brute paced in front of the door, his face bright red with anger as he kept clenching and unclenching his hands.

Caden handed him a glass of water. "Calm yourself and sit. Your head is bleeding, dope." She pushed him onto the couch and tore a piece off the flowery pastel curtains. After dipping it in the pitcher of water, she proceeded to clean his wound. "They got you good, didn't they?"

"Ehch," he grumped, turning his head.

She grabbed his chin and turned his face back. "Yeah, hero, stop pouting and behave. I'm not interested in fits. They're boring."

"What's wrong with Georges?" Teddy asked. "She drunk again?"

Ma rushed over and checked on her. "It's her heart. She's not strong, but she's resting."

"Any idea where Jolon might be?" Caden asked as she finished up with Henri.

They both shook their heads.

"Haven't seen him or Cate," Teddy said as he accepted a bowl of soup from Ma.

After wiping her hands clean, Caden tossed her rag in a corner and found a decent patch of carpet. "Cate is a survivor. If Jolon was near her when..." she paused, her thoughts flitting to Pa. "Well, she would make sure he was safe."

"So, what next step?" Henri asked, his grubby complexion pale. He propped his elbows on his knees and put his face in his hands. "What we do now?"

"We rest," Ma said, standing. She stuck her hands on her hips and eyed each one of them before turning her attention to the window where streams of light filtered in from an opening in the dirt at the top. "We are all broken and battered. No one can do anything in that condition. We rest. We wait, and we try to discover where we are."

"Ma," Teddy protested, but she dismissed him with a wave.

"No. I won't let any of you concoct some outrageous plan while you can barely stand. For now, we rest." She crossed her arms and patted her fingers against her elbows. "This place. This place is clean, cleaner than any place I've seen in Uppercity. Yet, I don't recognize it as part of the tower."

"Does anyone know how they found us?" Caden asked, as she stuffed a pillow behind her head and made herself more comfortable.

"It's hard to say. Cate and I went back through what I thought was the only other alternate route between Undercity and the mall, and there was no sign of anyone using it other than us. No, wait. One of the tunnels showed signs of use, but we thought that was some of the stragglers who didn't want to live in the tower." Teddy said, and Ma twisted around, her brows drawn together in anger.

"You and Cate went back? Went back where? When?" she demanded, standing over him.

"Ah, a few days ago," he said, his eyes wide with guilt. "We just went to check on things, see if anyone was trying to get through."

"Oh, you did, did you? And didn't feel the need to tell me? How dare you do something so dangerous?"

"Ma, we were careful."

With a dark scowl, she tapped his foot, making him yelp. "Yes, careful. I see that. Oh, I'm so tired of all of this." She slumped down beside Caden and stretched her legs out in front of her, crossing them at the ankles. "Don't tell me any more. Not for a while. I don't want to hear any more."

Cate slumped down on a mossy boulder and fluffed out her hair, scratching her head. It was a warm evening, sweet and fresh. The sky was clear and a half moon dangled in the deepening blue. "Okay. Anybody got any idea if we're getting closer?"

"Can't tell." Jolon dropped down beside her while Toro wagged his tail and stuck his wet nose against her hand.

"Everything is so green. I can't tell one building from another. Why is everything so green?"

"So, what are we supposed to do at night?" Nuna asked as she made herself comfortable in the grass. Toro thumped his tail against her leg and sat, his tongue hanging out.

"On the other side, we found a few shelters to hide in," Jolon told her with a weary sigh. "Can't make any out here. Not even a decent car to stretch out in. They're all rusted buckets covered in sharp, leafy plant stuff, that'll probably eat us if we get too close."

"Don't be silly. You realize there's a good chance we're lost?" Cate plucked a piece of grass and twirled it between her fingers. "Our rescue isn't so good, is it?"

"We're not lost, not yet." Toro came over to Jolon and licked his face. He scratched the pup behind the ears. "The buildings are still to our right. I'm thinking the greenhouses can't be too much further, but I'm not the adventurous navigator type. I'm more the bug collecting, cookie nibbling type."

As if to prove his point, he scooped up a long-legged bug hopping in the grass.

"The book Teddy gave me described this as a grasshopper. Strange things with big eyes."

"That's not helpful, Jol," Cate told him with an exasperated groan.

"He's just hungry," Nuna rummaged through her stash and handed them both a bar. "Weary too. We better find some sort of shelter before it gets too dark to see where we're going. There's no telling what might be out here."

"True," Jolon said as he munched. "Last time, I almost got eaten by a cat as big as Toro."

Cate got to her feet. "She's right. Though I'm not sure where to go. We don't want to lose sight of the buildings." She crossed the small square and discovered a path of broken pavement with weeds poking through the cracks. It ran parallel to the building and seemed easier to travel than the rubble filled path they had been following so far.

"I'm for checking this out. Maybe there's some place to hide out in further down."

Jolon joined her. "I guess. At least, the path seems clear enough to travel in the darkness."

"Right, then, forward you, young creatures," Nuna ordered, coming up behind them. Toro ran on ahead, barking with excitement.

Nuna chuckled as she went around them and led the way down the trail. "I think the outdoors makes him happy. This is better than I ever imagined. Are you sure it's safe? It feels safe, but it's terrifying too. Everything is so beautiful and fresh."

The path twisted and curved around, weaving them through the landscape. Everywhere there were signs of the past: rusted metal fences, broken plastic bins, and crumbling cars encased in greenery. Darkness crept in quick, and a strange creaking sound started up all around them.

"Frogs," Jolon said. "I think. Just going by what the books say, but it makes sense that it's frogs or toads." He swivelled his head around, peeking under bushes. "I'd love to catch one."

"Later, bug, this dark is getting creepy."

"Dark is dark, here or inside it's still creepy."

She glanced about. "Yeah, but inside has walls. This has open space. Anything can come at you from any direction in open space."

The three of them yelped as Toro jumped at them from behind a bush. He barked and yipped, dancing about them.

"Oh, you dumb animal," Nuna said, grabbing him and rubbing his sides. "You're supposed to be protecting us, not scaring us to death."

Toro ignored her scolding and trotted back down the path. They continued, only stopping when the trail ended at an alcove with glass walls and a shattered glass door. Massive vines with purple flowers dripped over the walls and metal frames.

"Do we go in?" Jolon pushed aside some vegetation and peered through the glass. "Can't see much." Tipper

The dog didn't wait for permission and plunged through the entrance.

"Toro, come back," Nuna hollered, patting her thighs.

"Don't think he's listening," Cate said and pulled a handlight out of her bag. She flicked it on and went inside, stepping with care on the broken glass. The shards crunched under her boots, but there weren't any other sounds than Toro's scampering about. The place was decayed and cluttered with broken junk and dirt.

"Watch out for ratdogs or other things," Nuna advised as they came in behind her.

"Bodies too," Jolon said. "Hate finding bodies."

Cate inched her way over a decayed pile of books. "Yeah, but the only bodies we'd find here would be decayed, skeletal ones. Looks like this used to be a bookstore. Teddy would be crushed to see so many books rotting away."

Something scurried over in the far corner. They whirled about; Cate shone her light and caught the red glint of rodent eyes.

"Just a rat," Nuna said, and Toro scampered after the creature. "Toro, leave it," she ordered as the rodent screeched and ran into a hole in the wall.

Wary of the unstable trash beneath her feet, Cate crept toward an opening that led to another room. The place stunk of mould and decomposing wood. There wasn't too much room for them to sleep even if they could get over the stench.

"There's another entrance back there." Jolon pointed to a spot where his light caught the outline of a large metal door. "Might lead to somewhere better."

"Yeah, and might lead to nowhere," Cate muttered, weary and disgusted by their surroundings. "Might as well give it a chance."

They worked their way toward it, and Nuna held their lights while Cate helped Jolon with the door.

"It's stuck and the handle's broken off," Jolon said, searching the exit for a weakness.

Cate pulled a piece of a metal shelf leg from the rubble and stuck it between the frame and the door. "Come on, bug, pry."

"I'm trying," he grunted as he tugged harder. "Don't think it's gonna move."

Nuna moved closer, shining her light on the handle. "Try there where the latch is."

They shifted the metal rod and shoved it in as far as they could. The door creaked, rust dust puffing out from the hinges. They pressed harder while Nuna propped the lights up and picked up a piece of stone. She hit the hinges, whacking them as hard as she could. The slab of metal collapsed with a scraping groan, falling back as they shifted away.

Coughing from the dust, Cate picked up her light and shone the beam through the entrance. "It's another hall, surprise, surprise."

Nuna stepped around them and went through with Toro by her side. "Actually, I don't think so. I think it's a tunnel."

"She's right," Jolon said, shining his light along the walls. "This is a scrounger's tunnel made in a caved-in building. See all the junk stuck in the rubble? Then there're these posts bracing the walls. This was dug out, and by the dust on the ground I'd say years ago."

"So it's a part of Undercity?" Cate asked, wiping the dust from her face.

Jolon turned about and wiped the sweat from his brow. "No, I don't think so. I think it might be a part of Uppercity. I would guess this area was scrounged right at the beginning."

"Okay, so we move carefully from now on," she said, bringing the metal rod with her. "There might be a place to sleep nearby."

"Or a whole bunch of trouble."

"We're not bountiful in choices." Nuna brushed a cobweb from her hair. "We could stretch out here for a while, but I'm all for going further to see if we can find something a little more comfortable."

"Comfortable would be good," Cate replied as she rubbed her arms. "Warm and safe would be even better."

Chapter 3

Teddy eased his foot into a better position; pins and needles coursed through his leg as blood rushed back in. Ma was asleep on the floor beside a snoring Georges, and Deb curled up on the couch, using Henri's lap as a pillow. The brute's head lolled side to side as he slept. Caden sat on a cupboard by one window. She leaned against the wall and hugged her knees, her forehead pressed against the window-pane as she peered up at the sky, her form silhouetted by the moonlight drifting in.

"Pretty sight, eh? At least, what you can see—a section of the moon and a couple of stars," she said as he hobbled over to her. "Can't believe they found us."

He hoisted himself up onto the counter. "Dorkas was a plant all along; I would guess."

She snorted. "Yeah. Dorkas." Her nails clicked as she tapped her fingers on the window. "This is real glass, not that unbreakable stuff, isn't it? Amazing it's still intact. What if we shatter this and left?"

Teddy blinked, why not? "Good question."

Caden swung her legs around and faced him. "No, why didn't we think of this before? We break the window and get out. They won't come in the room; they would be too scared."

"That's not a bad idea except we don't know where Pa is or the rest of the tower people. We can't leave them here."

She stared out the window again. "No, of course not. But outside is safe, right? We could escape and regroup. We could get Georges somewhere where no one can hurt her and get Deb away from the creepers."

He hunched his shoulders and stuffed his hands in his pockets. "That would be good. Ma too. Georges can't help us. Ma says she hasn't got the heart strength to go through much more. And Ma...."

"Ma what?"

They both turned; she stood near them with her arms crossed and a disapproving glower to her expression.

"Ma is not ready to believe your father is gone; is that what you're thinking? Or are you thinking I can't help get us out of here? I'm not helpless, children."

Caden jumped down and hugged her. "Of course not. You're one of the most amazing people ever."

She patted her on the head. "Thank you, dear, but hugging won't help us now. You've a sensible plan if we can go outside, but...." She wandered to the window, scanning the view as though she expected monsters to appear. "Is it possible?"

"Ma, you believe us. Just like that. No questions, no denial? We say we can go outside, and you believe us," Caden said as she came by her side and put a hand on her mother's shoulder.

"Oh," her mother began, her head bowed as she grasped Caden's hand. "I suppose if I wasn't so...I don't know what word is best. Exhausted seems inadequate. I grew up in the dark catching glimpses of the world outside. For a long time, I imagined walking out there and feeling the sun on my skin. After we moved to the tower, and I woke up every morning to the beautiful vista of a sunrise over a forest, I thought this is it. This is as close as I'll get. This is heaven and the future will be...well, there will be a future."

She turned and held Caden's gaze, her grey eyes bloodshot and bleary. "And it all fell apart. I've lost your father. We've lost everything. I have nothing left... no will... no ability to be surprised anymore. If we can get out and live or we can get out and we die, it doesn't matter. All that matters is we tried... we did something when there was nothing left to do."

"I break window," Henri said as he came over. "Take moment and we go." He pulled out his gun. "We use this if they follow. Then we get others to safety and find others."

"Perfect, we have a... thingy... pointy weapon..." Caden said as she gave her mother a hug.

"Gun," Teddy said for his sister. "Yes. Though we don't even know if the weapon's loaded. Or how to use it."

"Well, they don't know that either," Caden said, holding out her hand.

The brute's eyes went wide, and he shook his head. "Oh, no. Dangerous."

"No kidding." She rolled her eyes at him. "But you need to carry Georges and Ma needs to help Deb and Teddy. He can't walk and point this thing at anyone at the same time. So I'm the logical one left."

"She's right," Teddy said with Ma.

Henri hesitated before turning the gun over to her. "Careful. Handle here, trigger there. Don't point or pull."

She took the weapon by the handle, her face grim. "Okay, You get Georges. Ma, get Deb, and we'll figure out how to break the window."

Teddy hobbled over to the door and put his ear against the wood, listening. He held up his hand. "Hide the gun for a moment."

Caden tucked it behind her, and Teddy knocked on the door. Nobody answered. He knocked a little louder but still heard nothing.

"All right," he said, backing away. "Let's see if we can do this without making too much noise." He pulled the curtains closed. "We're going to need to move quick. Henri, put Georges over by that cupboard so we can slip her out fast. Ma, you and Deb stay by her."

Henri scooped the Upperlord up, and she groaned but didn't wake. "Oh, when she out, she out good." He propped her by the window, and Ma stayed by her side. Deb stood by her, sleepy and confused, but silent.

"Okay, everyone ready?" Teddy asked as he moved near them. They nodded and Henri picked up a chair while Caden pointed the gun toward the door. "Go."

Henri threw the metal seat against the window, and the pane shattered, glass tinkling everywhere. Fortunately, the curtain sheltered them from stray shards. Tossing the chair aside, he tore down the material and spread it over the sill, protecting them from getting cut.

"What's going on?" their guard exclaimed as he threw the door open.

Caden shut her eyes and yelped as she squeezed the trigger. The weapon jumped in her hand, and everyone jumped at the blast. The guard ducked back into the hall.

"Hell, they've got a gun. Get help," he yelled to someone they couldn't see.

Teddy hoisted himself up on the sill and flipped his legs over, gingerly putting his broken foot down on the grass covered soil piled up outside. Ma and Deb followed him, and he helped them down while Henri scooped up Georges.

The guard stuck his head back in, and Caden shot again, grasping the gun with both hands.

"Ah, don't stick your filthy bulbous head in here again," she said though she still appeared a little terrified of the power of the weapon in her hand. She backed to the window.

"Give me the gun," Teddy said, touching her shoulder.

"Uh, why?"

He rolled his eyes. "So I can cover the door while you get out."

"They broke the window; they broke the window." the guard exclaimed to people they couldn't see. "Air from the outside, it's getting in."

"Close the door," said someone Teddy suspected was Dorkas speaking in a squealing voice. "We'll die; shut the damn door."

"They've got a gun. They keep shooting."

"Close the door! That's better than dying from poisoned air," Dorkas squeaked again.

A hand reached across the entrance, and Teddy was tempted to shoot, but he caught the disapproving expression his mother bestowed on him.

"Let's go," she said, gazing apprehensively about them. The wind tugged at her hair, tossing the curls about.

"Go where?" Caden asked as they distanced themselves from the window.

"Good question," Teddy said, eyeing the area. The sun was low in the sky, and the air was chilly. The easiest way to travel seemed to be toward a half-crumbled brick building several meters away. "We might find a room or something in that building."

He slipped the gun back in Henri's pocket and accepted Caden's offer to help him walk.

She slipped her arm around his back, and they helped each other along. "So, that's a gun, hey?"

"Yep."

"Powerful."

"Did you like it?"

"No," she said with a sour twist of her features. "Too much power. The thought of killing someone with something like that or in any other way just isn't right."

"Not even Upperlords?"

"Not even them. I wish I had that kind of inner hate, but I don't."

"Me either."

By the time Cate and the others found a place to rest, she was tired enough to sleep anywhere. They found a tiny room with a useable door they blocked, so they could all recover without the fearing discovery by disgruntled Upperlords or their servants.

No one would find them here. The room and the hall showed signs of decay and neglect, implying years of lack of use by anything human.

Jolon slumped in a corner, stuffing his stash under his head and spreading his jacket over himself. He was asleep in moments, and she marveled at his ability to sleep anywhere.

Nuna discovered a pile of tattered rags and made herself a little nest. As she plumped them up, a dust cloud billowed out, making them cough.

"Come share," she said, patting a part of her nest. She wiped her hands on her sweater. "Not too clean. I don't recommend breathing, but they're better than the tiled floor."

Cate hesitated, but couldn't see anywhere else to rest. She sat down and stretched her legs in front of her, scratching her head. "Thanks."

"Ah, you're a suspicious one, aren't you?"

With a snicker, she turned toward the woman and arched her brow. "And you aren't?"

Nuna yawned, covering her mouth with her hand. "It wasn't a criticism, kitten. Just an observation."

They turned off the handlights, and the room became pitch black.

"Yeah, well, okay. I don't possess a high trust level," Cate admitted, her head aching. She rubbed at her temples and closed her eye. "Hate being inside now. There's no air."

"I can understand that," she said with a laugh in her voice. "Often, I imagined how wonderful life would be to be out in all that open and fresh air. And this is all just so much better than I could come up with."

"Yeah, I agree," she said sleepily. "I love it. Don't want to be anywhere else. Tired of tunnels and creeping about. This place, these buildings, they are death."

The woman didn't say anything; she just wrapped an arm around Cate's shoulders, and they both fell asleep.

When she woke, Cate flicked on her handlight. Jolon was still sleeping in the corner, and Nuna had curled up to the side of her with her head on Toro's stomach. She got off the floor, her legs and back stiff. A pressure in her lower abdomen signaled a full bladder. Frowning, she unlocked the door and peered down the hall. No one was around, and she doubted anyone would come along. Cautious, she slipped into another doorway and crouched, pulling her pants down. After relieving herself, she went back and found Nuna in a standing stretch with a handlight in one hand and her pack in another.

"Oh, that is a terrible way to sleep," she said, fishing out a bottle of water from her bag. "I'm not used to inconvenience like this anymore."

"Can't be morning yet," Jolon got off the floor with much muttering and stretching. "Oh, ouch," He grunted as he moved his neck about. "Not that I think I can sleep like that anymore either. I'll be back in a second," he said as he went out the door.

"There's a decent toilet area just off to the left," Cate told him. He waved thanks and disappeared in the dark.

"I'm low on food." Nuna passed her bottle over. "I think I have a couple more bars. Did you bring anything?"

She took a swig and passed the water back. "Didn't think of it. We kind of rushed out in a hurry. Maybe Jolon has something. He's always got food hiding somewhere."

"Usually," he said as he came back. "But the stash I brought is the one from Nuna's so it only has all the stuff she put in."

"That means there might be a few more bars and some crackers inside, but not much else."

"Oh, we make an excellent team." Cate took a bar from Jolon and ate, finding the food chewy, but good. "You make these?" she asked Nuna.

"Mh, yes," she said, biting into one. "They're a combination of a few things I discovered. One of the storerooms near the tower was part of a bakery, which has huge sealed tins of oats, raisins, dates, and sugar. You mix them with some water, and they cook together pretty good, little crumbly, but edible. Good energy too."

"Thanks for the cooking lesson. I'll have to remember it when I'm not stuck in a tunnel sneaking away from sadistic Uppers," Cate said though she didn't mean to sound so sarcastic. People were so awkward to be around.

"Yes, well, we should get going. The sooner we find the others, the better everyone will be."

Nuna tossed a bar to Toro and went out the door with Jolon following behind. Cate trailed after, wishing she could leave them and go back outside. "Damn you, Caden," she muttered.

Caden stumbled through the entrance of the brick remains of what must have been a pleasant home once. A broad, wooden staircase ran up one wall to another level, which was no longer there and the rooms on the other side were missing most of their walls, but she could tell how the place once was. She wove through the piles of bricks and lumber, stepping on a rug rotting in patches.

"This is not much of a shelter," she said to Teddy as he came beside her.

Her brother limped over a pile of brick, and she grabbed his arm as he wobbled on his feet.

"How about I check out the rest of the house, and you stay here with the others?" She helped him sit down. "I know you hate being the one left out of the exploring, but you're a hazard."

"I'll go with you," Ma said as she joined them. She nudged Deb toward Teddy. "Make sure he stays off that foot."

"Yes, Ma." Deb gave a two-fingered salute and plopped down beside Teddy, locking her arm in his. "You stay."

"I'm not a dog," he growled, his restlessness apparent on his face.

Deb stuck her tongue out at him. "No, you're my prisoner."

"Great."

Ma laughed and joined Caden, and the two of them went around a thick brick pillar and through an archway.

"This brings back memories," Ma said as they peered through the growing darkness. "Keep an eye out for glowing eyes."

"I think this was a kitchen. What memories?" Caden asked, inching her way along a tiled counter. Hardwood cupboards hung in the space above, their doors dangling from their hinges or missing altogether.

"Of scrounging. That's how I met your pa. I was scrounging through this one half-buried house, and I came across a box of kitchen utensils. He popped around the corner and grabbed my scrounge at the same time I did. He tried to take them from me, and I tried to keep them. After arguing for several hours, we decided to share, and that was the start of a lifetime of sharing."

She paused and sniffled, wiping at her eyes.

Caden rubbed her back. "We'll find him. Ma. We will. He's okay. I'm sure he is."

With a quick sniff, she donned a tight smile and nodded. "Right. So, this room might not be too bad. The ceiling's still good, and it's somewhat sheltered. There's enough room to make up a few beds if we can find something to use as bedding." She rooted through the cupboards. "Ah, that is what I was hoping for," she said, pulling out a couple of candles. "Now we just need to find some matches and a can or two to prop them in."

Caden pulled open a few drawers, shifting forks and spoons, and other kitchen supplies. "Got some," she said, holding up a pack. "Not too many, but they're dry."

"Let's give them a go," her mother said, taking the matches. She folded the cover back and struck the stick. It sparked, lighting up the room with a warm glow. As held the flickering match to the candle, the wick burst into flame.

"Ah, yes," she said with a long sigh. "Good. Hand me that glass over there."

Caden picked up the short crystal tumbler, and her mother dripped some wax in the bottom before sticking the candle inside. The tapered light stood and filled the room with a soft glow. She lit another candle and did the same with another tumbler.

"All right, now we can see what we're doing."

Caden went to the stove, opened the metal door, and pulled out one of the racks. "You think we can get a fire going in here?"

Ma peered in but didn't seem impressed. "Don't think so. But we could pile together some of the bricks in the other room and use the rack to cook on if we can find anything to cook. As much as I want to charge back into Undercity and find your father and the others, we need to take care of Georges and Deb first."

"Yeah." She went about piling bricks up until she had a relatively stable fire pit.

Her mother gathered up some scraps of paper and wood, placing them inside. She took one of the candles and lit the fire, blowing on the embers until the flames spread. Caden put the grate on top and secured the metal rack with a few more bricks.

"Well, that will keep everyone warmer. I'll get the rest of our poor group, and we'll clean out a bit to make room," Ma told her as she shoved some of the trash into a corner.

Caden dug up a couple of chairs and put them in front of the fire, the flames warming her fingers. One of the chairs had a broken back but was stable once propped against the counter. The other had a loose leg but was still useable. She flipped over a bucket to use as another seat and dug up a plastic bin for another.

Ma came back with Deb and Teddy, while Henri followed behind, propping Georges up as they walked. The Upperlord was awake though groggy and weak. He helped her to a chair, and she waved him away.

"Yes, yes, big brute. I'm all right."

Ma knelt beside her and peered into her eyes. "Fine? Georges, you had a heart attack. You're lucky you're still here. I have no medicine for heart failure."

"Eh," Georges said, waving her away. "Luck is a matter of perspective. I'm old, my friend, and nothing runs right. I feel air on my face. Where are we?"

"We're outside in a ruined house," Caden said, adding more wood to the fire.

"Oh, that's surprising. Is everyone outside, all of Uppercity or just us lucky rats?"

"Just us," Teddy said, grimacing as he sat down on the plastic bin, which sagged with his weight, but held.

"Why?"

They stared at her. "What do you mean, why?" Caden asked, her throat dry and sore.

"Why drag us outside? I mean this is pretty and all that. The air is breathable and," Georges sniffed, "fresh, but other than that how is this going to help?"

Caden rubbed her eyes as the smoke blew in her face. "Well, Teddy's wounded, you were dying, Deb's a child, and I'm not in the best of shape."

"Plus, we have no plan and only one weapon," Teddy added as Deb sat on the bucket beside him. He put an arm around her, and she slumped onto his lap with a dramatic sigh.

"We were like those characters in your stories, stuck, up the creek, whatever that is, sunk, in the pits..."

"Yes, Deb, that's enough," Ma told her, pulling over another bucket to sit on. "We get it."

"So, we're going to hide out here and what? Grow weeds?" Georges asked. "How long do you think it will take before they decide it's safe to follow us?"

"What difference does it make?" Caden asked, her voice gruff. "So they come outside. It's huge out here, and we don't need to depend on anyone else for anything."

"How many times must I explain this to you people?" Georges said. "They have no interest in freedom. They like control. If you take away their control, they will do anything to take their power back."

Caden threw her hands up. "And what can they do? Seal us in?"

Georges laughed. "No. Seal everyone else in, yes. But us? No, they'll just remove us from the scene."

"They kill us,"

Everyone turned toward Henri, who sat on the floor amid the dirt and rubble, his light brown hair hanging in a stringy mess over his face. "They kill us. We don't count."

"Finally," Georges gasped, pressing her hand against her chest. "Someone understands."

"Yeah, well, the problem with not counting to the mighty and important is you always count to someone else. And that's where the trouble starts," Ma said as she got up. "Henri, we need to make this a functioning shelter. Take one of these candles and see what you can find."

They moved Teddy about as they cleaned and tidied, trying to make the room somewhat liveable. Aggravated by his inability to help, he took refuge in tending the fire and watching Deb. She was so sleepy she kept drifting off on his shoulder.

After a while, Henri came back with a few blankets and pillows.

"Where'd you get those?" Ma asked as she took them from him.

"In basement. Shelves with plastic bins. Don't seem too bad. Some chewed by rats. Others good."

She patted his cheek and grinned. "Thank you. These are perfect. Any more down there?"

"I check. It not bad. Cold, but filled with stuff."

Caden took the blankets from Ma and wrapped one around Georges before handing one to Teddy and Deb. "Not too bad. If there're more pillows, we can make a few beds."

She went downstairs with Henri and came back a few moments later. "They had this thing—a bed of some kind." They laid out a vinyl square about the size of a double mattress. "I think you blow it up with air."

"Found pump. I think," Henri said, holding up a black thing with a tube and a squishable end.

"Yeah, you attach that end to the valve there and pump with your foot," Teddy said wearily. His ankle throbbed like it was trying to blow itself up.

Henri put the pump on the floor, and the others spread out the bed. He attached the end and started blowing the bed up, the pump making a wheezing sound.

"That will work for Georges and Teddy," Ma said.

Teddy glanced from the Upperlord to the bed. "Uh, I'm okay. Let Deb share. She's exhausted."

"Hey, boy, I don't bite. Though I do snore."

He mouthed a silent plea to his mom, meeting her gaze, and she relented.

"Oh, fine. It's probably a better fit anyway. Cad, let's search some more. Maybe we'll find a few more of these," Ma said and left with Caden.

After Henri finished filling the bed with air, he threw on a couple of pillows and blankets. Deb dived on first with a happy wheee.

"Okay, child. I can't take all that rambunctiousness. Let's remember I'm old," Georges said as she knelt on the bed. "Ho this thing doesn't feel stable, but I'm so tired I think I can sleep anywhere."

Despite her reluctance, she curled up on one side and wrapped a blanket around her. Deb settled in, staring at the ceiling and blinking until her eyes couldn't stay open anymore. Teddy threw more wood in the stove, stoking the fire high for the night.

"You good?"

He smiled at Henri. "Yes, I guess so. Just wish Pa was here. Do you remember what happened? I can't remember much. Everything happened in such a blur. I think he was still okay, but I don't know. Georges had blood on her, but was it Pa's? I'm so scared, I don't know what to do."

"Sleep."

"Yeah, good idea. Doubt that will happen."

"I need sleep." The brute yawned as though he was trying to swallow the world. "Lots of sleep."

"Me too," Teddy said though he couldn't stop his mind from dwelling on his father. His mother came back upstairs with her arms full.

"Well, there aren't any more beds, but there are some mats and more blankets. It's luck on our part that they stored everything in plastic bins. Don't know what we'd do otherwise. There are mouse droppings and chew marks on just about everything else. Smells too, like a sewer."

After the others had gone to sleep, Caden found herself restless. The night was chilly, but sweet smelling, and the half moon lit up everything in a silvery white glow. She wandered out into the other room and stood in the ruins. There were a couple of pictures lying on the floor, and she picked one up. The frame and the glass were broken, and the image had a few cuts across the faded surface. The family seemed happy, three children, two parents all cuddled with smiles, sunny faces, pristine clothes, and a unity that made her sad. She tossed it aside. It was all gone now.

Everything was always all gone.

Caden climbed on one of the broken walls and sat on the top. The wind played through her hair, an easy, gentle caress. The quiet was a soft blanket soothing her spirit. Everything was so different from the way she grew up.

People could go outside...live outside. How long had the entire population of Undercity and Uppercity been hiding behind walls when they could have been free? The emptiness of the question made her shudder. Why didn't anyone keep trying to get out? Why did they all just accept their fate and stay trapped within a dying world? Because it was easier, familiar. The answer sunk in her like a stone and overwhelmed her with sadness.

A leaf drifted down from a nearby tree, and she caught it. The texture of the bit of green vegetation was soft against her rough fingers.

"You like?"

Surprised, she jumped and almost fell off the wall. "Don't do that," she gasped, securing her seat again. "You scared me."

"Sorry," Henri said, his voice soft. The brute climbed up beside her and perched on a pile of bricks. "Couldn't sleep too."

With a long sigh, she gazed out on a field of rusting cars and decaying houses slowly disappearing under a carpet of vegetation. "Yeah. It's so quiet and beautiful. Scary."

"Scary?"

"Yeah. Unknown in a way that's intimidating."

"Ah," he said and shifted and inched closer, a warmth coming off of him that made her feel safe. His hands lay loose in his lap, and his chest rose and fell with every slow breath.

The urge to take his hand made her fingers twitch. She clenched her hands together in a tight grip.

A sparkle glinted in his forest green eyes. "I like out here. I could stay out here."

"Me too."

"Get you lots of flowers," he added with a chuckle, and a blush tinted his cheeks.

"Yeah." she said with a laugh and hopped from her perch, unsure of what she would do if she stayed with him for much longer. "But I guess we should sleep."

"You better," he said, joining her as she wove her way back to the shelter. "Your health better."

Pausing, she studied him, his stubbled, honest face, sincere. A warm sensation coursed through her chest, making her lips take on a soft smile.

"Yeah, I guess so, Outside is good. Easier to breath," she agreed, unable to say more. Somehow when she attempted to talk about anything personal with him, she vibrated with excitement and insecurity all at once.

"We okay, yes?" he asked, putting a hand on her arm then quickly taking it away. His brown eyes were pleading and insecure.

"Yes," she said, with a small grin. "Okay, you like me, and I like you too, but...."

"But?" he asked, his eyebrows rising with hope.

"But, I don't know. Everything is so temporary. We don't even know what's going to happen in the next couple of days."

"We could go," he said, sweeping a hand toward the open field. "We go and find new life elsewhere."

A deep longing gathered in her chest and rose into her throat as she gazed out at the field again. "Yeah, but what about the others? What do we do? Leave them?"

"No," he said, his face flushing with guilt. "No, we help get safe, then find nice home."

"How about we help get safe, and then we see," she said, with a frown as another rush of warmth confused her.

He seemed so sad and lost. She put a hand on his arm.

"We'll work it all out, Henri. I don't know what I want. I don't know what I'm doing."

"Me either," he said, running a hand through his hair. He backed away and smiled. "I go sleep."

"Me too," she said and went back into the other room. She curled up on the pillows in the corner and pulled a blanket over her.

A nice home—her mind filled with images of life outside and free—she and Henri building a home together with the others living nearby. This was a longing she never hoped to entertain before, and longing for it scorched her heart with a terrible pain. Tears poured down her cheeks. Happiness wasn't real, she reminded herself as she clenched her blanket in her fists. Why did everything have to be so complicated? Why were happy endings just a lie?

Chapter 4

In the morning, Caden woke early and went for a small walk. Her throat was so dry it was difficult to swallow. She explored along the side of the house and down what she assumed was a road. After a moment, she came upon a pretty walkway with a trellis covered in bright flowers.

Enchanted, she wandered down the moss-covered walk and onto the cement steps. Though ivy covered most of the building, the structure still seemed to be in pretty good condition. Wary of weak boards, she crept onto the porch, which stretched across the front, and stood before a weather-beaten door. Flaked bits of red paint peeling from the entrance showed the original colour of the fake, grey wood, and the surrounding brick was a pale sandy colour. Tentatively, she opened the door, which swung with ease, opening to a wooden floor and wide entrance.

The place appeared stable, so she inched her way in, testing the boards as she went. The house was not too bad. In the room to her left, was a fancy fireplace and a couple of couches beside two chairs. It was possible the furniture had mice and bugs hiding beneath the dull brown fabric, but the house wasn't too dirty. The walls were solid, and so were the windows. It was more like it missed the worst of the disaster, yet the owners left anyway. Or died. She shivered, not wanting to find any dead bodies.

Beyond the living room, Caden found the kitchen, which was spacious with lots of counters made of stone and several cupboards. The rotting scent of decay wafted through the room when she opened a large white appliance. With a quick shove, she closed the door and waved her hand in front of her nose. A hundred years later and rotten food still stunk when sealed away.

As she searched through some of the cupboards, Caden found a bunch of cans and packs of dried goods. This was good. They needed food. Some of the cans were bloated, but a few seemed useable. She picked up a bottle and worked out the words iced tea as she twisted the cap off and sniffed. It smelled okay. She took a drink the liquid soothing her dry throat. With a quick flick of her wrist, she tossed the empty bottle aside and grabbed a pack of cookies and ate a few.

She had to get the others. If all went well, they could take shelter here for a few days until they figured out what to do. After grabbing a few cloth bags from a shelf, she loaded up on some supplies and headed back to the others.

Ma was up and scrounging through the cupboards when she got back. Henri was awake too and working on keeping the fire going.

Caden dumped her sack on the floor. "Got food and stuff to drink," she said, opening the bag. "Some cookies, something called iced tea, crackers, and something like cereal cakes or something like that."

"Where did you get all of this?" Ma asked, taking a bag of cakes from her.

"I went for a walk this morning and found a home not far away. The place is in decent shape too. There's a fireplace in the living room and several couches. The walls are sturdy and the thing seems sound, which is amazing. I didn't go upstairs to check on the rest, but the kitchen has lots of food 'n stuff we can use. Doesn't seem to be any sign of mice or lots of bugs. Whoever lived in the house, sealed the building up tight. I found some ants in the kitchen, but they only seemed to get into the stuff that wasn't sealed."

"You went by self," Henri said, frowning at her. "Not safe. You should wake me."

"I've been taking care of myself for a long time, brute. I know how to sneak about and stay safe." She tossed him a bag of cookies. "You're welcome, by the way."

"So, this place, we could stay there?" Teddy asked, sitting up on his makeshift bed.

"Yay, breakfast," Deb said, diving into the bag.

Ma tugged on her shirt and pulled her back. "Slow down, child. Sit and I'll get you some food. Caden, could you check on Georges and bring her one of these drinks? They're not too bad."

"Sure, Ma." She grabbed two cereal cakes and a bottle before she went over to Georges' bed and knelt down.

The Upperlord snored and snuffled, her braids sticking to her mouth and covering her face. Caden shook her arm, uncertain of how to wake the woman up.

"Umm, Georges? Breakfast."

She snuffled and snorted before rolling over.

Caden shook harder. "Come on, food. Yummy food and something to drink."

"Drink?" Georges gasped, brushing tangled strands of hair from her face, her eyelids opening and closing as though she couldn't quite get them to open. "Where?"

"Right here, though I think you'll be disappointed. It's basically water with a bit of something settled in the bottom. Bottle says Iced Tea. No alcohol."

The woman made a face, but sat up and yawned, her face contorting in the strangest ways. She twisted her features into one of disdain but took the drink. "Sure, fine. Tea. You are trying to poison me."

"No, she's trying to help you," Ma said as she came over and examined the Upper. "You're looking better. Your colour's better, and your eyes are much more clear. How's the heart?"

"Tired," she said and bit into a cereal cake as though she was eating wood. She munched for a moment and tilted her head to the side. "Not bad. Might go down okay. So, you found a shelter better than this, did you?"

"I thought you were asleep." Teddy took the cap off a bottle and sniffed before taking a sip.

"Asleep, I still hear everything." Georges stood, a little shaky on her feet. "All right, let's go see this home of yours. As much as I appreciate this blown up bed, it gets a little soft by the morning, and your little doll of a girl squirms."

Ma wiped her hands on her trousers and pushed her hair out of her face. "Okay, if you think you're up to moving. Henri, help Georges and I'll lend Teddy a hand."

Caden took Deb's hand, and they left the ruins behind. The sun was out, warming her skin. She smiled despite their situation.

With a shiver, Ma turned her face toward the blue sky. "It's endless. I thought the sky windows of the sunshine room were fantastic, but this. Oh, your father would love this."

Teddy hugged her as they hobbled along. "Don't worry, Ma. We'll find him and get him back. Then we'll bring him out here. Everything will be right again."

In the warmth of the morning light, they made their way to the gate all dripping with fragrant flowers. "Oh, how beautiful," Ma gasped, touching one of the bright red blossoms.

"Yeah, the place is a bit of a fantasy, isn't it?" Caden said, gazing at the two-story building covered in vines. She led them to the door and went inside. "The house doesn't stink too bad. Musty, but clean, considering.

While Ma helped Teddy to one of the couches, Henri guided Georges to the other.

"Not a bad home," Georges said, tucking a dusty pillow behind her head. "Imagine what this place was like before the world blew up."

Ma propped Teddy's foot up on a short table. "Don't like to think about it. The past is so far away; I would rather not get caught up in trying to recover it."

Cate snuck down the hall and made her way through the gloom. The passage was stinky with little air and a dank fragrance as though water seeped into everything. Nuna followed behind her, and Jolon took up the rear. Where they were going, she had no idea. Nor did she have any clue as to what they were looking for.

"Seems to me finding the Upperlords is not the best of ideas," she said, turning sideways as she paused at a corner. "What are we going to do if we find them?"

"Good question," Nuna said, holding Toro back as the dog tried to rush forward. "Behave, pup."

"I don't know, but I think the best thing to do is try to find the others first," Jolon said, slipping in front of them. "If we can do that without getting caught, maybe we can get them out and get away from all these Upper creeps."

"Not bad," Nuna said, tilting her head in thought. "We need to be quiet and make sure no one sees us."

Cate laughed; the sound echoed down the hall. "So we sneak about Uppercity searching for them, right? Terrific idea. We don't even know if this is going to lead us to Uppercity."

"Stop being negative," Jolon said, his round face flushed. "I'm hungry and tired, and I miss my family, so I don't have much patience for putting up with you."

Aggravated and miserable herself, Cate leaned toward him, grabbing his shirt. "How about I just leave you here, then? You don't need me. You've got all the answers."

"Why don't you?" he spat back, his face twisted with bitterness.

"I just might," she growled back, her gaze locked on his.

"Oh, come on, you two. I know you both are worried and upset, but this is getting us nowhere. Now. Let's keep going." She shone her light down the path to the left. "I think there might be a door this way, and I'm about ready to find out where it's going."

"Fine," they said together, glaring at each other.

Nuna and Toro led the way, and the old woman paused for just a moment before opening the door with care. Weak strands of light drifted in. The three of them leaned in and peered through the opening.

Beyond the door was another hall, which was clean and showed signs of being used on a regular basis. The grey tiles were chipped and cracked but swept of all dirt. A row of round, flat lights ran down the ceiling. No one seemed to be about, but the air was better, and several other doors dotted the walls down the passage.

"Come on," Jolon said, pushing them forward.

"Careful," Cate told him as she stumbled out into the hall. "If that's your idea of sneaking about, I'm surprised you survived this long."

"Sorry, I just want to find my family."

Nuna patted him on the shoulder. "I get that, boy, but she's right. We need to be a little more careful. I'm going to assume from the lights and how clean this area is, that this is your Uppercity, but there doesn't seem to be anyone around."

"Pa always said that most Uppers don't get up until much later in the day, so they're probably all still asleep," Jolon said with a half shrug.

"Huh," Nuna snorted and wandered down the hall. "Well, if that's the case, this might be easier than I thought."

"If we're lucky, we might just be able to blend in with the crowds," Cate said as they went. Along the way, she tested a couple of door handles, but they were locked.

"Have you ever been up?" Jolon asked as they went.

"Not really," she said with a frown. "Been to the market, but I managed to avoid the rest."

"How?"

"Eh, not an interesting tale," said Cate as snippets of the past distracted her thoughts.

"I've heard stories," Nuna said. "Some of them pretty dark. I find it difficult to believe some of them are true."

"They are," she said with a snort. "Oh, yeah, they are. The Nest, the Adult Quarter, the Brute rings, they're all real. Well, the Nest isn't anymore, but I wouldn't be surprised if another sinkhole has taken its place. I grew up in the Nest. So did Caden. We hid in the fringes, but there were lots of creepers around waiting until the time was right. Caden was never strong, and so they didn't think she would live. Those Uppers left her to die in the tunnels. Me, they thought I might serve, but my attitude was a bit of a drawback. I wasn't subservient enough. Wasn't quite pretty enough to make up for it. Made it easier to escape. As soon as I could, I snuck away and found Caden where they dumped her. I managed to get her to the Northern Side, hoping I could find a place where she could live—someone to take care of her. She was so weak. Almost died. We had taken care of each other since we were old enough to be friends."

"So you're the one who got her to Ma and Pa?" Jolon asked, the compassion on his face annoying.

"Yeah, well, didn't make sense to me that she should die because of the creepers. They seemed good enough. I watched them for a few days before I brought Cad to their warehouse. I left her by the door, and they took her in. Didn't bother her much after. Didn't want to. She was happy. She got better. That's all I wanted. And why I'm telling you all this, I don't know. I think I'm a little nervous wandering about here. These people terrify me."

"Understandable," Nuna said, her worn face sad. "Well, that's enough dribbling on about the past. Don't matter much. Nobody can change it." With a slow exhale, she grasped Cate's shoulder. "We better keep moving."

"Right," Cate said, turning from the older woman's piercing gaze and compassion. Instead, she shoved the sadness and pain of her past away and tried another door. The handle turned with ease. She held a hand up, and the others stopped beside her. Cautiously, she inched the door open, peering inside. It was a small apartment, which appeared to be empty.

They slipped inside. The room was pretty with shelves of books, flowered furniture, and bright windows. A tidy kitchen stood off to the left. To the right was an alcove, which contained a huge bed framed with wooden pillars draped in thin white material.

"Wow, this is quite the fancy place," Nuna said, going to the window. "Looks out on a pretty park too. Wonder what person lives here?"

"Good question, but who cares?" Jolon asked, searching through the cupboards for some food. With a crow of delight, he pulled out some baked goods and handed some to each of them.

"What?" he asked as Nuna raised an eyebrow at him. "I'm hungry. We have hardly eaten since yesterday, and I don't care if it's stealing or not. These people have been taking from me all my life. They can suffer."

"I'm good with that." Cate took a big bite of the rectangular pastry, which was flaky and sweet with gooey insides.

"This is a strawberry," Nuna said after she took a bite. "Mmm, I remember this from before the tower when I was just a child. We had found a trove of them in a patch where no one thought anything would grow. My father thought they were poisoned because they grew near the outer walls, but that didn't stop some of us from eating them. Hunger has a way of making one try anything. Where did they get these, I wonder?"

"Good question," Cate said, helping herself to another pastry. She wandered over to the kitchen where a large white appliance hummed. A cool blast of air hit her when she tugged the door open. The shelves were overflowing with food: eggs, chicken, and a myriad of vegetables she had never seen before. "Where did they get all of this?" she asked, turning to the others.

"This is a little more than a few chickens and potatoes," Jolon pulled out a round red vegetable and took a bite. Juices dribbled down his chin. "Yum."

"This is disgusting," Nuna said as she examined the appliance. "This is a fridge, a working fridge. Even with the power we've managed to get going in the tower, there was never enough to run a refrigerator. Always tripped the breakers."

"These Uppers were hiding a little more than the sun from Underlings, weren't they?" Cate closed the door and went to the stove and turned a dial. The burner in front of her lit up, singeing her fingertips as she touched the swirling metal. "Ouch. This sucks. These people are horrible."

"Well, it's about time they shared," Nuna said and went over to a closet by the bed and rummaged through the clothes hanging inside. "Here." She handed a dress to Cate. "Slip this on."

She held the blue slip of material by the corner with two fingers. "I don't wear dresses."

Nuna took out another long dress in creamy orange and went into the little room by the other side of the bed. "We need to blend in, and this is the best way I can think of. I don't know who lives here, but they probably won't be gone long," she said through the open door. "Hey, you know, this bathroom works? Everything, even the toilet."

"So, Upper has plumbing like the tower." Jolon said. He rummaged through some of the drawers and found a clean shirt.

"Yes, but their water is clean, really clean."

Cate went in the room and turned on the tap. She cupped her hands together and took a sip. "Of course, they send us second-hand water while theirs is clean and sparkling."

Nuna closed the door and began taking off her clothes. "Doesn't make much sense. We've gotten the quality of water and essentials to quite a high level in the tower, but nothing like this." She drew the dress over her head and adjusted the material on her body. "Not bad," she said, smoothing the fabric out. "Come on, get changed."

Rolling her eye, Cate tugged off her shirt and trousers and pulled on the dress. The garment was a bit big, and she had to double wrap the sash, but the cloth was soft and clean. She studied herself in the mirror and Nuna handed her a brush.

"See if you can tame those curls. We need to look respectable," she said, emphasizing the word respectable with a tinge of hate.

"Well, it's going to take a little more than grooming and clean clothes to make us look like anything more than Underlings," she said as she tugged the brush through her red locks. She finally surrendered and tied all her hair back, securing the bunch with a stretchy elastic band. Turning back to the mirror, she made a face at her fancied image. "They're gonna notice my eye and Uppers don't have such limitations."

Nuna whipped out a dark green scarf decorated with blue flowers and wrapped the material around her head, covering most of her missing eye. "There you go, lovely girl, beautiful, but not noticeable unless someone gets close. And if they get that close, a swift kick in the shins will distract them."

Cate laughed. "Hey, you're not bad, you know that?"

"Thank you. I try. Let's see how the boy is doing?"

Jolon stood by a desk searching through the drawers. He had changed into a clean shirt and a jacket, which fit him well enough. The pants he put on were a bit long but serviceable.

"Well, we might just pass if nobody peers too close," Jolon said.

Toro trotted over to Nuna, sniffing her clothes. She patted the dog on the head and rubbed behind his ears. "Do Uppers own pets?"

"They own everything else, so I would think so," Cate said, flipping through some of the books. "Everything here is in such good condition. I don't get it."

"Who cares?" Jolon said as he went to the fridge and pulled out some of the meat. He took a strip and held the morsel out to Toro, who gobbled the food up. "I'm sick of them. Let's find the others and get as far away from these people as we can."

Cate took a glass out of the cupboard and turned on the tap, filling the glass with cool water. "Agreed," she said and took a long drink. If we keep our heads down, we might be able to get around without being caught."

They stuffed their clothes in Jolon's stash then left the room, tidying up as best as they could to hide their presence. After they stored their packs in the scrounger tunnel, they made their way back.

Chapter 5

C aden and Henri went upstairs, unsure of what they would find. The wood steps creaked but seemed stable enough to hold their weight. Three doors lined the hall. The one to the left was open and light streamed trough in dusty rays, and the other two across the way were closed.

They checked each room, but didn't find anything scary or dangerous: dusty furniture, comforter covered beds, dressers with clothes still in the drawers, and personal items such as pictures, figurines, and toys. The ceiling in the far bedroom showed signs of water damage in one corner—recent, something possibly fixable.

One room contained a charming yellow bed with big blue flowers scattered over a comforter. Deb would like such a room. There were pictures of cats and horses pinned up on pale yellow walls, and white furniture with gold trim.

"I scrounged through lots of wreckage, lots of people's lives. This place is odd to wander through. It's like they walked out and left everything as it was," Caden said with a shudder. A creeping sensation went up her spine as though ghosts were following her.

"Maybe they weren't home?" Henri said, picking up a stuffed penguin.

"Probably out shopping." Caden shuddered, thinking of all the bodies they had discovered while scrounging.

"Hey, they might been survivors. We might stand in the house of somebody's great, great grandparent, or something."

"Don't talk about stuff like that, Henri. The dead are the dead, and the past is the past. At least, I hope so." She sat down on the bed and fluffed the heart pillow. "What are we going to do?"

Henri handed her the penguin and sat down beside her. "No ideas." He was so close, and he smelled good like the wind in the trees.

Unsettled by his presence, she leaned away. "You should go get Teddy. Ma wants him to rest for a while. He won't like it, but we'll plop Deb in here with him, and he can read some of these books to her. We'll put Georges in the other room so she can rest too and Ma can take care of them while we explore a bit."

He nodded and left, returning moments later with an annoyed and complaining Teddy in his arms.

"Put me down. I can walk, I can," Teddy said and Henri plopped him on the bed. "Look, I can, ow!" He yelped as Caden tapped him on the ankle.

"Yeah, you can lay there," she told him, flicking the blankets over him. "And stop whimpering. I barely touched you."

"Hey, books!" Deb exclaimed as she came in. With a quick skip, she plopped in front of the shelves and rummaged through the rows of new novels. After collecting a pile, she plopped them beside Teddy and scooped the penguin off the floor, hugging it. "This room's comfortable. I like it." She snuggled in beside him and flipped open a book with teddy bears in coveralls. "This one looks fun. I'll read it to you, so you can see how good I'm getting."

"In a moment, okay?" Teddy asked, taking the book from her. "Could you go downstairs and ask Ma for something to drink?"

"K," she said and hopped out of the room.

"Hey, Henri, you want to go bring Georges up?" Caden suggested as she caught Teddy's eye.

"So what's the trouble?" she asked, sitting beside him. "Aside from the fact that you're frustrated with being useless."

He put the book aside and spread his hands over the blanket. "My foot's getting better. At least, it was before you decided to help. You and Henri, you both are going to go back, aren't you?"

"That's the idea."

"You sure you're up to it?"

"What do you mean?" she asked, her face blank and innocent.

"You know what I mean," he said with a roll of his eyes.

Caden got up and went over to the dresser. Little figurines, pictures, and other items cluttered the surface. She played with a bright stone with letters carved in it.

"I think being outside helps," she said, rubbing her thumb against the smooth surface. "I still get moments of weakness, and there is always a headache lurking in the back of my skull. But, you do what needs to be done, don't you?"

"That's why I should go too." With a grunt, he attempted to toss back his blankets, but got his leg caught up in the folds.

"Yes, that's like using a piece of wool for a walking stick," she said with a chuckle. "Henri may be big, but I think he can only handle one broken person at a time. I may have my moments, but you can't walk and if you insist on walking, it won't heal. So no, you sit there and take care of Ma and Georges. I'll be fine. Henri will be with me, and we're going to do some scouting around to check what's up."

"Fine," he said though he pouted as if she had taken away his favourite food.

Henri came back in and handed her a pinkish grey stash with an odd colourful horse on it. "Your ma filled with stuff. Got me one too," he said as he gestured to the blue pack on his back decorated with some sort of smiling greenish blob. The stash was so small he could only sling it onto one shoulder. "Says we can't stay out long or go far. She worries."

"Yeah," she said and waved to Teddy. "We'll be back before dark. If we're lucky, we'll find something life altering."

"That would be wonderful."

Cate stumbled as they walked down the hall toward the crowd of people gathered in a bright square.

"Careful," Jolon hissed as she grabbed his arm to steady herself.

"You try walking in shoes like these," she said, wiggling her black shoe at him. "They're too big and these stupid heels. How do people do anything useful in these?"

"Shush," Nuna said as a couple rushed past them. "We're trying to blend in."

Cate pushed her way around the edge of the crowd, trying to discover what was going on yet remain unnoticed.

"Well, now we know why no one was in that apartment or the halls. Everyone's here," Jolon whispered.

"Why?"

"Good question. They're like rats, and they congregate when they think something's going wrong."

"Listen," Nuna said and gestured toward a large platform in the middle of the room.

The five people standing on the stage looked stern and unhappy. One of them was the Belinda person who took over the tower. Her black ropes of hair were twisted up on her head, her dark suit made her seem even more severe, and her white smile stood out grim on her night-black skin. Beside her stood the Dorkas creeper with his weasel face and gritty clothes. They were having a heated discussion with three other people, a short pale woman in grey pants and a flowery blouse, a tan person with a rough beard and a silver dress, and an old man with white-streaked hair, olive skin and wearing a silky grey robe as though someone interrupted him in his sleep.

"This can't be good," Jolon said, peering around a tall woman in a red hat.

"All right, enough." Belinda raised her hand toward the crowd. "Many of you heard the rumors, but I'm here to tell you that is all they are, rumors. There is no need to panic or worry. No one broke any windows. No one exposed us to the unfiltered air of the outside. We are safe. I assure you."

The crowd rumbled and mumbled, but the man in the robe beside Belinda donned a benevolent smile.

"Please, let's all go back to our business. We are safe, and we will continue to be so. I believe one day we will step out beyond these walls, but that day is not here yet. The readings are still too dangerous though they are getting better with each passing season." He turned toward the short woman. "Cataza has monitored the conditions outside for years, as her family did before her. You trusted her; you trusted us for all your lives as your families have. Trust us now."

Belinda surveyed the crowd with compassion etched in her expression, nodding her head. "Now, please, my fellow Upperlords, go back to the pleasure of your days."

"Well, aren't they wonderful," Jolon said as they moved behind a large sign advertising some kind of restaurant.

All around them, people of different shades and shapes moved on, talking amongst themselves. Everyone appeared pleased and relieved.

"Come on," Cate said as their cover began to thin. "We need to blend in. The crowd is disappearing, and we better too."

"Which way?" Nuna asked.

Several exits branched off in different directions. Cate caught a glimpse of Belinda and her group disappearing down a narrow hall across from them.

"Come on," she said, motioning to the others. "Let's see what they're up to." She stepped out from behind the store, taking on the haughty expression of the Uppers around her while Jolon and Nuna followed behind.

Once she reached the other side, she slipped down the hall, keeping several steps behind Belinda. They wove their way through several doors and up two levels of stairs, getting farther and farther away from the safety of the scrounger tunnel they used when they first entered Uppercity. Carpet covered the stairs, but she worried that they would be caught if anyone glanced behind. Luckily, none of them did.

When everyone reached the second floor, they went through a set of double doors and down another hall with bright cherry doors. They stopped at the second one and went inside. Cate rushed behind them as quietly as she could and caught the door just before it closed.

The others piled in behind her, and they hid by the side of the entrance while she peeked inside. Beside the front door was a small closet containing a couple of long coats and a pile of old shoes. After, the apartment opened up to a sunken room with windows along the outside wall. Cate motioned to the others, and they pulled back.

"I'm going to sneak in; you two wait here," she whispered to them.

Nuna looked as though she was going to protest, but Jolon nodded and pulled on the woman's sleeve. Cate snuck around the door, easing into the closet. The Uppers were not too far away, and she poked her head further into the hall, crouching close to the floor.

"Belinda, speak up," Cataza said, tapping the side of his head. "Can't hear, can't hear."

"Oh, I'm already shouting," Belinda said as she sat down on a brown leather couch and draped one leg over the other. "Since we lost Magistrate Tipins, the level of trust among our fellow Uppers has diminished."

"Ungrateful, that's what they are," muttered Cataza.

"So, these rebels, they went outside," the old man in the robe said. "You are certain." He turned a cold eye toward Dorkas as though addressing a bug.

"Yes, they smashed the window and escaped." The creeper shifted from foot to foot. He dropped himself into one of the chairs and bounced back out as Belinda scowled at him.

"I told the guards not to say anything; told them they died."

"Did they?" the man with the beard asked as he poured some kind of gold liquid into a clear glass. "I'm hungry, what are you serving for snacks, Belinda?"

"I dismissed the servants, Torres, so nothing. The fewer ears listening in, the better." She turned back to Dorkas. "And my sister was with them?"

The creeper nodded. "Yes. The rebels took her with them. Don't know if she was conscious or not. The brute was carrying her. Only caught a glimpse of them for a moment before they disappeared in the dark. Didn't want to let the death air in, so I closed the door and sealed the room."

"Fine, Dorkas. That's enough. Why don't you go into the kitchen and make yourself useful," Cataza said, dismissing him with a wave of her long fingers.

After he had left, the others were silent for a moment. Cate thought that she might leave them where they were, but then the silver dress guy began to talk.

"What are we going to do, Belinda? We are treading on very tricky ground here. If this tower is as good as you said it is, then we could lose our subjects."

"That won't happen, Ueno."

"Why didn't we leave the rebels in this tower? No one knew about them and what do we do with them now?"

"Yes, we could have left them there to become stronger, to cultivate a rival city that could draw away all our people and resources."

"Why are you worrying about the tower?" Torres asked, pacing. "I'm more concerned about what might happen if people think they can go outside. We might have a mass exodus. We might lose everything."

"Yes, everything. That's what you are worried about," Ueno said, whacking him with a stick. "What about your life, you dope?"

"Ahh, hey. What are you doing?" he demanded, limping as he rubbed his shin. "What do you mean, my life?"

"If people believe they can go outside, they'll start opening windows and doors. Poisoned air will flood in. We will all die."

"Cataza, how dangerous is the atmosphere outside?" Belinda asked, her fingers pressed together and elbows propped up.

The other woman's expression soured. "Please. Don't ask me. I haven't been able to get a proper reading in years. Most of my equipment is broken, and no amount of scrounging has turned up any replacement parts. I would get better results stealing those crude testers from the scroungers than relying on my gear, but I'd still need to go outside to use them."

Torres snorted. "Just grab one of those rebels and toss them out. If they live, we're safe. If they die, who cares?"

"We would still need to open a door to throw the bugger out," Ueno said, his brows twisting together in annoyance.

"Enough," Belinda said, standing. "I'm weary of all of you. Go. Before I throw every one of you out."

Before she could be caught, Cate scooted out the door while Belinda's guests gathered themselves together.

"They're leaving," she hissed at the others, and they hurried down the hall and around a corner. They ducked just in time as the door opened and the Uppers filed out.

Cataza caught Dorkas' sleeve. "Get rid of the rebels. Take them to the sewers. Dump them down the doctor's pit in that room under the market he keeps for failed experiments. Chop them up and feed them to the Underlings. I don't care; just make them disappear. The last thing we need is more rumours stirring people up."

"That's a lot of people to store. I don't know if there's enough...."

Torres dismissed him with a wave that almost clipped his head. "Enough what? Throw what you can in the freezers and toss the leftovers in one of the empty halls near the pharmacy. They might be able to put the remains to some sort of use." He linked arms with Cataza. "All of this is tiresome. Let's go back to my greenhouse. I cultivated an unusual new plant and acquired a tasty wine."

"Sounds splendid." Cataza sighed. "Sounds perfect. All this strife is boring. I don't understand why some people can't just go on in peace. They have a place to sleep and food. We leave them alone. Why must they cause trouble?"

Jolon traded a disparaging glance with Cate as the Uppers disappeared down the hall. Dorkas headed toward them, so they pulled back, trying to blend in with the walls. Cate held her breath, hoping he wouldn't turn down their way. Luck was with them as he kept going straight and she signalled the others to follow him.

They kept their distance and kept him in sight as he wound his way through the hallway and down another set of stairs. He went through a set of yellow doors guarded by two brutes, and they stopped halfway down a flight of steps, just out of sight. Careful not to make noise, they inched their way back up and into the hall where they wouldn't be discovered.

"Perfect. What do we do now?" Jolon asked, leaning against the wall. He slid down and pulled out a pack of bars he had taken from the Upper's apartment. "All this sneaking is making me hungry."

Nuna paced with Toro at her heels. The dog was well behaved: following every order and keeping to her side.

"I'm going to assume the people you all had brought over to the tower are the ones Dorkas is supposed to take care of, but what is the pharmacy?"

Cate shrugged, and so did Jolon. "Never heard of it. I don't understand much of what these Uppers do. There's a darkness, a disgusting emptiness and superiority hiding in all of them."

"They live in fear," said Nuna. "I knew such narrow people in the community I came from. I believe the initial catastrophe divided the people into the capable and the needy. The needy became dependent, incapable of surviving without help. A hundred years of control fortifies the position of your Uppers."

Nuna sat down beside Jolon. The dog rested its head on her lap. "Their life is pretty sweet right now. They get the best of everything, and they don't do anything to obtain it, except make certain everyone stays in their place."

Cate slumped down beside them. "So, what now? We can't follow Dorkas, and we have no idea how this stupid part of Upper works."

"At some point, we'll be discovered. There aren't enough Uppers to hide behind," Jolon added, handing her a bar.

She took off the wrapper and bit into the dry snack. "Hide. Yeah, we should find a place to hide."

"We could go back to the scrounger tunnel," Nuna suggested, rubbing at her temples. "That might be our best bet. It's a ways away from here, but nobody goes there. Then we can find out a little more about our surroundings."

"It's a good idea," Cate said. "But I think we should keep an eye on this place too."

"I'm going to stay." Jolon gave a half shrug. "Those Uppers told Dorkas to get rid of the others. If he went this way, that means they're somewhere this way too. Can't get past those guards, but I can wait and see if he brings them back through this way. I'll be able to hear the guards coming up the stairs, so I can hide a level above. And I can watch through the stairwell."

"Sounds good. While you're doing that, I can probably make my way to the market, blend in, and snoop about. I might pick up some useful information."

"This world is unfamiliar to me, so I don't know how much help I can be," Nuna said.

"When I was in Belinda's apartment, they said that some people escaped by breaking a window. I'm thinking one of those people must be Teddy. It seems like something he would do. Sounds like Georges and Henri are with him. Maybe some of the others are too."

"You think?" Jolon asked, his eyes hopeful.

"Yeah, there's a good chance. So I was thinking, Nuna, could you go back outside and see if you can find them?"

"Outside? Outside is huge. Where do I start?"

"All right. It's not the best plan, but we need to know for certain who got away and who is left to rescue. Maybe we can snoop around and find out where they escaped."

Nuna frowned at her but nodded. "Fine."

"Good. Jol, I'll meet you back at the hideout tonight. Don't disappear, or get caught, or anything," Cate told him and he donned a sarcastic grin.

"Ooh, are you starting to care?" he asked with a fluttering of his eyelashes. "Don't. It scares me."

Let's go," Cate said and got off the floor.

They left Jolon and wound their way back to the Upper Square. Only a few people wandered around, and none of them seemed interested in anyone, but themselves.

Nuna sauntered over to a trio of ladies with dogs. "Ah, what a fine puppy," she exclaimed to a narrow woman with a tan complexion, a flower-filled blue dress, and a fuzzy grey pup in her arms.

"Thank you," flower lady said, giving a broad smile. "Your dog is quite lovely."

"Oh, thank you," Nuna said, petting Toro behind the ears. "I've had him all his life. My mate gave me him as a puppy."

"Large dogs are so rare. Where did he get him?" asked the round, hairy woman holding a dog so bushy it was difficult to see its eyes.

"Oh, I never asked. I always find it's better not to ask, if you know what I mean," she answered with a laugh and a wink.

"No, I don't," hairy dog owner said, but flower woman nodded, her tight curls bouncing.

"Yes, that's sometimes the best thing to do."

"Where are you from?" hairy woman asked, her grey eyes narrow and her pale face bitter. "I've never seen you around here before." She gave Nuna the once over. "I would remember."

"Oh, that's because I don't go out often. Bad heart. Keeps me from doing much. That's why my partner got him for me." She jerked her thumb toward Cate. "And the girl, here attends to me."

"Not bad," said the third squat woman with ruddy skin similar to Nuna's. "I have one too, helps me with my sight, which isn't so good," she said, placing a hand on Nuna's arm. "Handy most of the time, but there are several drawbacks."

Cate clenched her teeth, but Nuna nudged her with her foot.

"So, what brought you out?" hairy woman asked, and Nuna took on a horrified expression.

As she donned an apologetic smile, she placed her hand on her chest. "Oh, I heard about the window breaking. It terrified me. I had to find out if it was true."

"Isn't that awful?" flower lady said. "I had nightmares last night just imagining what horrors that might bring."

"Where did they say it happened?" Nuna asked, lowering her voice and making her eyes wide. "I don't know Uppercity very well. Spent most of my life in my apartments, and I'm so afraid of stumbling into the wrong area."

"They say it's somewhere near the greenhouses down that way," squat woman said, pointing to a hall just behind the platform.

"Where's your partner?" hairy woman asked, her dog yipping as she petted the animal aggressively.

Nuna scanned the room. "Oh, he wandered off somewhere. I'm supposed to meet him here at some point, but these men when they get talking. I probably will need to go find him."

"Well, you can just visit with us and wait for him here," flower lady said, and the other two women exchanged a nasty glance.

"Oh, dear, that won't work," exclaimed squat woman. "I'm afraid we must go. Important lunch date. So sorry, dear, we'd invite you along, but it's an exclusive appointment, invitation only. Come along, ladies. We don't want to be late."

"Sorry," flower lady said with a hand on Nuna's arm. "Protocols. So tiring, but what can you do? It keeps us alive."

"What do you mean? What keeps us alive?" Nuna asked as they followed behind the other two women.

"Oh, come now," said hairy woman, turning back. "You can't be that isolated."

"My husband doesn't tell me anything. He believes it might affect my heart. Please, tell me. I'd love to know. I don't want to do anything wrong," Nuna said in such a pleading, apologetic voice, the woman relented and Cate had to swallow a laugh.

Hairy woman rolled her eyes but donned a superior smile. "The protocols of Uppercity that govern our world were set up soon after the disaster."

"In the beginning, when the food ran out, people went beyond insane," the flower lady cut in as though she was enjoying herself.

"Folks began eating each other," squat woman said in a whisper.

"Yes, as I was saying, things fell apart." hairy woman said with a disapproving glare for her friends. "The division of Undercity and Uppercity was necessary to gain some control and achieve a certain level of normality. All the protocols and rules we have now keep people in their place and give them a sense of purpose. If anyone could go anywhere, how would you know who to trust?"

She let out a mocking laugh. "Can you imagine having those Underlings to tea? They'd steal everything you had before you could offer a cookie."

Squat woman nodded sagely. "Yes, and probably murder you too."

"And that's why invitations are so important." Hairy woman gave Nuna a scathing glance. "Can't have just anyone show up." She turned toward the others and gestured with her head. "Come. We'll be late."

After the Uppers had left, Nuna and Cate drew away from other people.

"Well, that was hateful," Cate said, wishing she could throw something at hairy woman.

"Yes, but helpful."

Cate grinned at her. "Well, you're quite the performer. I'm impressed."

"Oh, blending in has always been a good survival skill to cultivate. In my old world, I found it to be very handy when trying to find out who is on your side and who wants to gut you."

"Yeah, I get that," Cate said, appreciating the woman more and more. "Normality, what's that? Seems like a terrible excuse to put yourself above others."

Nuna gripped Cate's shoulder. "Yes. I'm going to see if I can discover this broken window. What are you going to do?"

"I'm going to see if I can find out how the people in Undercity are doing. See who's still alive and on our side. They plan on killing those who came with us to the towers. We are going to need all the help we can get to prevent that from happening."

"Be careful," Nuna said with a pat. She turned away, and Toro followed behind as always.

After she had left, Cate tried to figure out which way led to the market. She turned about and picked a hall they had not explored. It was the busiest exit and seemed the most logical choice. Covering her nervousness in a quick step, she wished she could pull her hair over her face and hide. Fortunately, nobody paid her much attention.

Chapter 6

Teddy sat in the frilly bed and stared out the window. Deb had left to help Ma collect water from a rain barrel in the backyard. After they strained and boiled the water, they would be able to drink it. Fresh water, fresh air—it all seemed like an illusion.

A tree whipped its branches against the glass, scratching the surface. He flipped back his blanket and hopped over to the bench by the sill. Dappled sunlight and a myriad of flowers filled the front yard.

Farther up the street, lumps of rusted vehicles lay up the road, and the houses on either side were either falling apart or taken over by greenery. One or two seemed to be in about the same condition as the one they had moved into. Others showed burned out signs of fire. Several streets down, shapes of other buildings stuck out of the ground—high towers broken and crumbling.

A moan and a thump came from the other room.

"Georges?" he called and got no answer. Grimacing, he used the walls to make his way to the other room. "Georges? You alive?" he said as he pushed open her door.

The Upperlord lay on the floor with her feet splayed in front of her and a weary expression on her face.

"Oh, yeah," she said, tugging at her braids. "Ah, my hair got caught under me. Happens every so often." A heavy sigh escaped her as her shoulders slumped. "I've had this hair forever."

"Well, that makes sense," Teddy said, bracing himself against the bed and helping her up. "Most people have had their hair since they were born unless they go bald. Then I guess they might borrow some from others or wear a hat."

"Clever. I've never cut it." Georges ran a hand down the length of her hair. The braided strands of grey and black reached well past her waist. A long exhale escaped her lips as she shook her head. "Don't want it anymore. Too much. Tired of work and life and pain."

Amused, he raised an eyebrow at her. "See, words like work are not ones I associate with you. No offence. I don't associate it with any Upper."

"Ha, ha," she said as she stretched back on the bed and pulled a periwinkle blue comforter up to her chin. "I suppose if I compare it to scrounging, my life seems lazy."

"But it isn't?"

The Upperlord grinned and shrugged. "Who can say? I'm tired, so I did something."

Teddy shifted to the other side of the bed and propped his throbbing leg up. "Me too."

"The chore of growing up with Belinda was not easy. She is so much like our parents: driven, cold, individualistic. See, they had a strange way of detaching from those around them as though they were inanimate objects." A low groan escaped from her as she leaned forward and adjusted her pillows. "One time, this Upper woman who used to be my mother's constant companion mentioned that her servant had developed a terrible and incessant cough, their solution was to get a new one.

I never understood them. For a long time, I thought I was some baby they took from some other mother, except my nose and eyes are like my father's. And I got my father's feet." She stuck her foot in the air. "Big.

I used to sneak food to the kids the Uppers keep to clean the streets at night. I convinced my parents I had a huge appetite and burned everything off. Belinda hated me for that 'cause no matter what she ate, she gained weight. I don't know why it mattered. My sister was considered the ultimate catch of Uppercity."

Teddy laughed at this. "Really? I can't picture that. Such bitterness doesn't seem that appealing to me."

"Hand me that water over there, would you?" She gestured to a mug on the side table. He passed her the cup, and she took a long drink. "Mmmn. Thanks. The old throat gets so dry."

"Probably all that alcohol."

She snorted and waved a hand at him. "Didn't drink as much as people thought. The drunken fool worked as a wonderful ruse to get me into places where Belinda wouldn't find me, and I could get all the info on both Undercity and Uppercity."

"So, you didn't drink much? You're good at pretending," he said with a wry grin.

"Okay, so I drank a bit too much sometimes, but sometimes life was all so..." she held her empty hands out in front of her, palms up, her face slack and her eyes clouded with sorrow.

"Yeah," Teddy said, understanding what she meant. The low, empty ache he carried in his heart all his life throbbed, reminding him of the many dark days in the tunnels.

"It was stressful sneaking food and medicine to those in need... people like your family and people like Henri. The challenge of staying under Belinda's radar was an interesting task. As children, she liked to follow me and snitch on everything I did. Her squealing didn't make me many friends, and I acquired many enemies. I never realized just how much stress my secretive endeavours caused until we lived in the tower, and I had nothing to do. It was the strangest thing. The first few days there weren't too bad, but then I unwound like a spring. Sent my body into twitches. Literally—I shook and everything. Your mother insisted it was withdrawal. Maybe. Whatever the reason, it left me tired."

"I never realized you did so much. Pa always said you were a good person."

The woman laughed heartily at this. "Oh, your pa. He's one of the good ones."

"So you believe he's okay."

"Your father?" She paused, her face going slack. Worry creased her brow as her fingers clenched the comforter. "I choose to believe so, but then, I've done so all my life."

"Done what?"

"Choose to believe the positive despite all odds. It's my way of pretending everything's fine. Keeps me from jumping into a pit."

"I'm glad you didn't, jump into a pit that is," he said with a pat to her shoulder. "None of us would have survived without you."

Georges frowned but looked pleased around the eyes. "Get out, kid. I need to sleep."

He chuckled and crawled out of the bed. "Yeah, me too."

Chapter 7

Caden stumbled over a shifting pile of rocks, and Henri caught her by the waist.

"Hey." She slapped his hands.

"Sorry. Didn't mean hurt." He stuck his hands behind his back, his face tragic.

"Don't worry, you didn't hurt me," she said more harshly than she wanted. "I'm just not real big on being touched."

"Didn't want you to fall," he said, shuffling his feet as they went.

She groaned and punched him in the arm. "It's fine. Thanks. I appreciate your concern, okay?"

"Okay. Next time I walk in front, then you fall on me, oh!" he said, turning red.

Laughing, she shook her head. "Don't worry. How about I just keep a hand on your arm? Then I won't fall, and you won't need to catch me."

"K," he said with a grin though the rest of his face looked disappointed. "Where we going?"

With a hand over her eyes to shield her vision from the sun, she studied the area. They had been walking away from the house for quite a while, following the remains of the street. Many of the houses they passed were beyond repair.

"There's a small path that way," she said, pointing to a place that diverged from the road and into a well-treed area. "Might be good."

"Trees. Dangerous?"

"I don't think they attack," she said with a chuckle. "Don't know about cats, though."

He patted his pocket. "Still got gun. We safe."

"That thing is scary," she said, rubbing her shoulder. "I think I pulled something using it."

"I need to practice. Shooting it, that is. Don't shoot straight. Not many bullets, though. That's what Teddy said they were. Bullets." He glanced back down the path. "How far we go?"

A soft gurgling sound caught her attention as she paused to listen.

"I think there might be water running that way. Sounds like water. Not that I've heard much water except the stuff that comes out of a tap, but it has a watery sound. Kind of like the fountain back in the tower."

The lines of his square jaw tightened as he donned a serious expression and nodded. "Water, yes. We go explore?"

Hiding a grin, she kept going. He wasn't a horrible person. The more she was with him, the more she liked him, she just wasn't sure where to go with the whole romance thing. It always sounded so yucky and pushy in Teddy's books. The girl gets to wait around wondering if the guy likes her or the guy forces her to like him despite herself. She hated that kind of thing. Yes, she wanted a friend, a partner, and even a kiss or more, but she didn't want to lose herself to get it.

"Hey, look," said Henri, pointing toward a gushing stream.

The water was beautiful, sparkling in the sunlight as it wove through the trees. "Wow. That's incredible. And loud," she said, laughing. She knelt down and let the liquid run over her fingers. "Cold too. Do you think it's safe to drink?"

"Hope so."

Something jumped not far from her, and she fell back with a yelp. "What was that?"

"Umm, don't know." He pulled out his gun and held the weapon in his shaking hand.

"I don't think it was dangerous."

"Might be. Might be bad."

Though her knees protested, she stood and put a hand on his arm. "I think we're safe. You can put that away."

A crimson flush ran up his neck to his cheeks as he chuckled and tucked the gun back in his pants. "Cautious."

"Yes, never hurts to be cautious," she said with a lingering touch to his hand.

The brute gazed down at her, his green eyes passionate. Her breath caught in her chest, creating an aching tightness to her throat. The unexpected intensity of his expression excited and terrified her. As he stepped closer, he clasped her hands, and she shivered from the contact.

In the corner of her vision, the creature in the water leaped again. Caden grinned with a delight intensified by her mixed emotions. "Wow. I think that's a fish, a real fish," she said, taking the opportunity to change the topic. She pulled away, rubbing her hands on her arms to release the tingling warmth from his touch. "They are gross, but they're supposed to be good to eat."

"They are."

Both of them swirled around at the sound of the other voice. Henri fumbled for his gun, but Caden stopped him.

"Wait," she said, taking in the new arrival.

The woman standing in front of them was older, deep brown in complexion, and muscular with a dark red scarf wrapped around her head, hiding most of her hair. A wild, fresh quality hung about her as though she spent most of her time outside. And she smiled kindly, all the way from her full lips to her dark golden eyes.

"Didn't mean to scare you," she said, her hands at her sides as though she was calm but ready to move if she had to. "I've been watching you for a few minutes." She put a hand up. "Not in a killer way, but in a curious way. I haven't seen another person in so long; it's good."

Caden eyed her with caution. "Where did you come from?"

"Oh, I don't know. I used to live in a tall building with a fountain and such, but I went exploring and got lost. Wasn't such a good move, but I got caught in a storm. How about you? I am assuming you both are friendly. You are friendly, yes?"

She and Henri traded a glance. "Yes. I guess we are, friendly that is. We, ummm, well, we came from this house over that way," she said, pointing back toward the house. "My mother and brother are there with another woman. Ma can be a little cranky and Teddy's a bit annoying like brothers can be, but they like people for the most part."

Caden stopped as she realized she was giving away too much information. Nervous, she moved closer to Henri. Why was she sharing so much? This woman was a stranger, unknown. But there was something about her that seemed so easy, so unthreatening. Despite this, she reminded herself to be more cautious.

The stranger nodded. "I have some of that fish if you are hungry. We could share."

"Never had fish," Henri said as his stomach grumbled.

"Right. Well, it's quite tasty. The water's drinkable too. If you need some, help yourself."

Caden shifted around, unsure of what to do next.

"Why don't I collect the fish from my trap, and we can bring some to your mother. I'm sure she'll like them. Grilled over a fire, they taste delicious, especially with roasted vegetables."

The woman went over to the bank and pulled up a rope hidden in the long grasses. As she drew the cord out of the water, she pulled up a cage woven out of branches. Inside, fish squirmed and wriggled, fighting to escape.

Despite her fears, Caden moved closer to the creatures, fascinated by their strange appearance. The skin seemed slimy, and the goopy eyes stared as their mouths worked back and forth.

"So, what do we do?" Henri whispered as they stood apart from the stranger while she worked. "We don't know who she is or anything about her. What if she dangerous?"

Caden put her hands to her hips and tugged on her bottom lip with her teeth. "She doesn't look too dangerous. I think you can take her. Plus, we have the gun."

"Course I can take her," he said, frowning with offence, before his eyes widened in confusion. "No. Don't want to take her in any way."

The distress in his voice made her chuckle. "Relax. I think we will be okay. She's clearly been living out here for a while, and she has food. Those are two things in her favor. Hopefully, she might be able to help us figure out what to do."

"Might be more than her."

While they watched from a safe distance, the woman clubbed the fish with a stick. After, she pulled out a crude knife and cut into the flesh with practiced ease.

"Depends if her story is true or not," Caden said. "Guess we'll find out soon enough."

"All right, let's go," said the woman as she stood up with a string of dead fish in her hand. "Lead the way."

Teddy sat up in his bed as he heard the others returned. The afternoon drifted by in small naps and long stories despite all the attention Deb wanted.

"They're back," the little girl exclaimed as she ran out of the room.

With a bit of effort, Teddy worked his way onto his feet and hobbled to the top of the stairs. His ankle was stiff, but the swelling had diminished considerably. He paused, listening. There was a new voice with them, one he did not recognize.

Careful not to put pressure on his foot, he made his way down the stairs and into the kitchen. A sturdy woman with black hair, a loose grey sweater, and coarse, baggy pants stood by their mother, offering a handful of what he recognized as fish. Ma stared at the creatures as though they were dangerous.

"Ah, thank you," Ma said as she took the fish from the woman. "I, uh, well. They are interesting."

"Would you like me to cook them?" the stranger asked. "Fried fish is a specialty of mine, and I'd love to treat you."

"Fine," Ma said, handing them back. "I'll, um, see what I have to go with them. I found some canisters in this little closet over here. Might be something."

The woman grinned, her teeth white like Georges though her skin was several shades lighter. Her nose was broad and lips full, and her eyes sparkled a bright gold.

"Check for rice. I found some in a few different houses. Cooks easy and is terrific with fish."

"Rice, right," Ma said as she went to the cupboard. She glanced Teddy's way with a skeptical frown. "Shouldn't you be off that foot?"

"Hey, Teddy, what you doing up?" Caden asked as she and Henri stopped staring at the newcomer and turned his way. "This is, uh, sorry, you didn't say what your name was."

"Right. It's Jemma," she said with a salute in Teddy's direction. "Nice to meet you. You must be the brother."

Deb stepped out from behind Henri and stuck out her hand, blowing a strand of her blonde curls from her eyes. "He is Teddy, and I'm Deb. Those things are yucky. Are they okay to eat?"

Jemma wiped her hands on her shirt and shook Deb's hand. "It's good to meet you, and yes, they are delicious. Just you wait. I'll make you a feast."

"So, you said you came from a building that was like a tower and had a fountain, is that right?" Caden asked with a side-glance toward Teddy.

The words made his eyebrows shoot up. The stranger couldn't be Nuna's lost spouse. No, but then, who else would she be?

Jemma plopped her fish on a board, took out a knife from a drawer and started to prepare their meal. She sliced the heads off and pulled out their spines complete with thin bones. After, she put them in a pan and rummaged through the cupboards.

"Yes, I did. I lived there with my wife." The woman paused her expression dimming. "I never meant to leave her. I just went too far and couldn't find my way back. Then survival became a priority." With a deep inhale, she shook herself and went back to her fish.

Teddy went to say something, but Ma put a hand on his arm. "That's too bad," she said as she put a bag on the counter containing tiny white kernels. "I found your rice stored in a metal tin, so it's good."

"Perfect," Jemma said. "Best way to cook rice is via steam, but for now, we can just boil it in water."

Meanwhile, Ma took a pot from a cupboard and poured some water in it from another larger pot. "Boiled this earlier. Henri, could you check the fire in the other room? We'll need some wood to keep it going. There are several dead branches in the back yard. Please collect some more. Caden, please go up and check on Georges. And bring her some fresh water."

They both left, and Deb followed Caden, skipping around her as they went.

Ma picked up a bowl with tiny blue berries in it. "Deb collected these this morning. I think they're edible, but I'm not certain."

Jemma plucked one from the bowl and popped it in her mouth. "Tasty," she said with a wink. "Though sometimes you might get a bitter one that isn't quite ripe yet. It's amazing how much we forgot in a hundred years, isn't it? In language, food, mechanics, science, and more, we've fallen so far we don't know what's edible around us anymore."

With a tentative smile, Ma tried one of the berries before passing some to Teddy. He took a couple and put them in his mouth. The flavour was as refreshing as stepping outside right after the rain. After licking his lips, he took some more.

"Save some for the others," Ma said, putting the berries aside before passing him the bag of rice and picking up the bowl again. "Can you manage that?"

He nodded and followed both of them into the living room.

"It is wonderful to talk to people again. How long have you been here?" Jemma asked as she stirred the fire and set up to cook.

Ma propped up the pot on a few bricks and shoved some coals under it. Once she coaxed the embers into flame, she poured the rice in the water and put the cover on.

"We just found this place this morning," Ma said, her tone wary.

Teddy sat back and lifted his leg up onto the couch. He didn't know why his mother was being cautious, but he didn't want to get in her way. If the woman was who he suspected she was, she was no threat to them.

"Ma, Georges wants to come downstairs," Deb shouted as she ran down the stairs. "She's being ornery and doesn't want any water either."

"It will probably cause less stress on her if she comes down than if we leave her up there," Teddy said as Henri came in with a pile of wood.

He dumped his load by the fireplace, and Jemma stuffed a piece in with the coals.

"Yes, I suppose," Ma said, sitting in a high-backed chair. She stared at the fire as Jemma tended the fish. The scent made Teddy's mouth water.

"I help get," Henri said as he went to the steps.

Deb climbed on Ma's lap and hugged her. Her pale blue eyes were sparkling with tears. "I love it here, Ma. Can we stay? If we find Pa, can we stay? It's so fun to go outside. I can't go back to the tunnels. They make me sad."

Ma kissed her on the forehead. "We'll see, love."

"It is difficult to go back," Jemma murmured as though she was thinking of something else.

Moments later, Henri came down stairs with Georges in his arms and Caden close behind them. He placed the Upperlord on the couch and offered Caden another high-backed chair. She smiled at him awkwardly but sat down while he shuffled about the room.

"And who are you?" Georges asked, eyeing their new guest.

"This is Jemma," Ma answered for the woman. "Caden and Henri came across her this morning. She was out fishing."

Whatever silent conversation went on between Georges and his mother as they faced each other, Teddy couldn't guess, but neither of them seemed all that ready to trust their new arrival.

Jemma dipped her chin Georges' way. "Good to meet you. All right, this fish is just about done. Let's see how the rice is doing." She lifted the lid to the rice and stuck a spoon in the pot. "Not bad. Definitely edible. Everything seems ready to eat."

"I'll get plates," Caden said, and Henri trailed after her.

They came back with a tray of dishes, which they passed around while Jemma served each of them a good helping of fish and rice.

Teddy sniffed the food, the steam rising to his nose. His stomach rumbled as though it was tired of waiting. He glanced over at the others who were all poking about their plates.

Jemma laughed and dove into her meal, juices from the fish running down her chin. She wiped her mouth with a cloth she pulled out of her pocket. "Good stuff. Don't worry. I've never poisoned anyone in my life, and I'm not about to start now. People are too hard to come by to get rid of."

Caden collected the dishes when everyone was done and brought them into the kitchen. She stacked them by a pot of warm water and washed them off before rinsing and stacking them on a tray of wire.

"Need help?" Henri asked, showing up beside her with his hands full of dishes.

"I need something," Caden said, scrubbing the fish pan. "Can't say what, but I definitely need something."

"You upset."

She bit back the smart remark on her tongue. "Yeah, I'm upset." After wiping the soap from her hands, she rubbed her eyes. "We're wandering around making a pretty home and gathering up strays while Jolon and Cate are missing, and Pa could be..." She choked on her words and thrust a plate into the water. "I need to do something."

"Me too." Henri slumped against the counter as he dried a pot. "So what do we do?"

"Uh, Teddy's out of commission and Georges is not much better. That leaves you and me." She wiped her hands on his towel and gazed up at him. He was so broad and muscular, yet his face was gentle and his green eyes as deep as the forest surrounding them.

"I guess it's up to us."

"Uh, huh," he said, his mouth soft and his gaze riveted on her.

"Henri, Caden, Ma says to come back in the living room," Deb said as she came skipping in the room.

Caden blinked and stepped away from the brute, tugging at her hair. "Ah, yeah. I'll be right behind you." She kept her gaze away from Henri's. "You go, and I'll finish up and be right in."

The brute tossed his towel aside, his expression dazed. "Sure. Good."

Deb caught his hand in hers. "Come on. You can carry me on your shoulders."

Obediently, he scooped her up, and they left.

As she leaned against the counter, Caden took a moment to gather herself together. This was the completely wrong time to get gushy over a guy, especially a muscular, sweet, loving guy who was slowly turning her heart to mush. She clenched her teeth. No. There was too much to do.

"Caden," yelled Deb from the other room.

"Yeah, coming," she yelled back.

High on a shelf by the sink she found a tin container marked tea. When she pried off the lid, a light sweet scent emanated from the crushed leaves within. A quick search of the cupboards led to a teapot, which she filled from her mother's bucket of purified water. After, she placed the pot on a plastic tray along with some teacups and left the room.

"Found some tea." She placed the platter on a table beside the fire and poked at the leaves. "Seems decent. I thought I might make us some."

Her mother smiled at her as she put the teapot on the brick props and stuffed some red coals underneath. When she finished, she scooted in beside Teddy, keeping as much distance as she could from Henri. "What's up?"

An uncomfortable silence descended on the room. "Well, umm. That was an excellent meal," Ma said as she sat across from Jemma. "Thank you, for the fish."

"You're welcome," the woman said, pursing her lips after. She studied each of them and smoothed out her baggy pants. "Well, have you decided if it is a good idea to share with me the reasons why you all are here, or not?"

Georges laughed. "And I thought I was straightforward. Since I know most of them, I do believe you are not an Upperlord, am I correct?"

The woman blinked. "I'm not even certain what that is, so I wouldn't be able to say if I was one or not."

"I would say that answers that, then," Georges said as she tapped her fingers against the couch. She glanced over at Ma. "I don't suppose it would hurt to tell her. It's not like sharing the information will change our situation much."

Ma frowned thoughtfully, pushing her blonde curls away from her face. "I guess not. Fine."

She proceeded to tell of Uppercity and Undercity, sketching out detailed descriptions of their society and the people in it.

Caden exchanged a glance with Teddy as she left out any information about the tower and their recent adventures there. He made an almost imperceptible shrug, and they both remained silent. Ma did share about the confrontation between the Uppers and Underlings, and the shooting of Pa, but she made the event sound like it happened in the warehouse.

"Well, that is incredible," said Jemma as she took the cup of tea Caden offered her.

"Incredible?" Ma's eyebrows drew together. "You make this all sound as though it's a story I made up."

"Oh, no. Sorry. No," the woman said, putting her hands up in front of her chest. "I believe you. It's just I can't believe I've been living out here for so long just a short distance from such a community. So what do you plan on doing now if you don't mind my asking?"

Georges sighed heavily and put her teacup on the table. "That is a terrific question. Seems to me we can either stay here and get on with living, which is something I don't think any of us can do." She added the last part hastily as everyone started to protest. "Or some of us have to go back and see if we can find those we've left behind."

"Which is something you are not able to do," Ma added before she pointed at Teddy. "You either. Neither of you would be any help."

Teddy opened his mouth to protest, but slumped back on the couch and nodded, crossing his arms over his chest. "Fine. Guess that leaves Henri."

"And me," Caden cut in. "I'm all right," she said as they gave her a skeptical once over. "Completely fine."

"Well, I will go, if that will help," Jemma offered, and they all stared at her. "Don't get all prickly. It's a genuine offer."

"So that's it, then. The three of us will go," Caden insisted with a particular glance toward her mother.

Ma nodded, staring at her teacup as creases of worry surrounded her eyes.

Two hours later, Caden, Henri, and Jemma approached the room they broke out of. The sun was high in the blue sky, making the day hot. All was quiet. No one seemed to be around, but they proceeded with caution. As they came close, they huddled behind some bushes.

"Do you see anything?" Jemma asked as Caden peered around a leafy branch at the building.

"No, nobody's here as far as I can tell. The window's still broken, but I don't think anyone's in the room. Stay here. I'll check it out."

"Careful," Henri said, his expression all dopy with worry.

After giving him a reassuring nod, she crept through the grass until she reached the window. Her ears strained to hear anything human. Careful not to cut herself on the glass, she peered over the sill. The room was dim and difficult to see in, but she couldn't make out anyone about. She crept back to the others.

"Seems empty, but it's dark in there so go slow. Someone might be hiding in a corner though I doubt it. The door is closed, and the place looks like it hasn't been touched."

"So we go in?" Henri said, standing.

Caden tugged on his arm and pointed to all the other windows surrounding them. "Hey, wait. Who knows who's watching?"

"Well, this is interesting," Jemma said, gazing about.

"Is anything familiar?" Caden asked as Henri crouched back down.

The woman shook her head. "No. I've never been this way before. At least, I don't think so. I'm pretty good at mechanics and such, but directions are a bit beyond me."

"All right, well, no matter who might be watching, we can't just hang out here all day. That's a perfect way to get noticed."

Caden went back to the window, and the others followed her. Henri helped her over the sill. Her boots crunched on glass, and she moved to the side so Jemma could get in. As a shudder inched up her spine, she ran her hands down the sides of her pants, dreading entering Uppercity again.

"I check door," Henri offered, going over to the entrance.

In case of trouble, Caden and Jemma stood on either side of the frame. Not that Caden had any idea what she would do. She searched around for a weapon, and all she could find was a plastic tray.

"Don't open it."

"Oh, crap!" she exclaimed in reaction to the voice coming out of the shadows in the far corner. "Who's there?"

"It's me, Nuna," she said, stepping into the sunlight. She stood there in an orange dress with uncomfortable looking footwear on. Her face kept fluctuating between shock and joy and anger, her eyes glued to Jemma. Toro let out a bark and jumped forward, tail wagging as he greeted the other woman as though they were old friends.

"Nuna," Jemma whispered, taking a step toward her. Absently, she scratched Toro behind the ears. They traded a glance that was difficult for Caden to describe.

"Jemma," the other woman gasped. "I... you. You're alive."

"Yes," she said, taking another step.

"And here."

"Yes," said Jemma and stepped forward again, her hands outstretched. "And here."

"With me."

Jemma took the other woman's hands, tears in her eyes. "Yes, with you."

Nuna shook herself and slipped a hand away. Her lips tightened as did her eyes. She slapped the other woman across the face. "Where have you been? If you were that tired of me why didn't you just say so? You've been outside all this time?"

"I'm sorry," Jemma exclaimed, her tears running down her face. "I didn't mean to. I... I got lost."

"Lost," Nuna repeated with disgust. "That's it? You got lost?"

"Yes," Jemma said as Nuna turned away. She moved toward her, putting a gentle hand on her shoulder. "You know how terrible my sense of direction is. I never meant it to happen. I just ended up outside one day. I was going to go get you, but I wanted to make certain the way was safe first. I wandered a little too far, and rain started to pour. I tried to get back, but the storm turned awful, and I couldn't see well through the wind and rain. I scrambled to find shelter, determined to get back to you when it was all over, but I went too far and lost my way. I searched and searched, but I think the more I searched, the farther away I got."

She waited, but Nuna wouldn't look at her. "Please, love. I'm so happy to be with you again. I missed you every day I was out there on my own."

Nuna's back convulsed with a disparaging chuckle. She whirled around, jabbing a finger at her wife. "You missed me? I missed you. I had no idea what happened to you. You just, you disappeared."

"I know."

They faced each other in silence before embracing each other, their tears mingling as they kissed. Toro circled them both, rubbing against their legs and yipping.

Caden turned away, wiping her tears away with her sleeve.

Henri cleared his throat. "Why no open door?"

Nuna stepped away from Jemma but kept her fingers locked with her wife's. "Guards patrol the hallway. I only managed to slip in here when they had already passed. Took a bit to unseal it in a way that would make the seal seem intact when closed. Almost got caught."

"How did you end up here?" Caden asked, plopping onto one of the chairs. Her legs ached with all the walking, and she was weary.

Jemma and Nuna sat down on the couch clinging to each other as though they expected one or the other would disappear if they let go. Toro sat at their feet, his tail thumping against the floor.

"You not prisoner?" Henri asked as he stood behind Caden's chair.

"No," Nuna began, her face serious. "I came here to your Uppercity with Jolon and Cate."

"Jolon and Cate? They're alive?" Caden asked, her heart quickening, and she leaned forward. "They're okay?"

Nuna rested back against the couch. "As far as I know. Jolon is watching a passage that we think leads to the other Underlings from the tower and Cate went to the market to try to find out what your Uppers are doing. Seems they plan on removing anyone who went to the towers."

"Of course," Caden said, bitterness settling on her tongue. "They are the only ones who count, after all."

"Yes, well, many of the other Upper citizens wander around in blissful ignorance while a select few do as they please. Anyway. I followed some rumours about a broken window and made my way here. Took me almost the entire day to sneak past the guards and get in here, but I was just standing about wonder what my next move was when I heard you coming. I figured it might be you, but I wanted to make certain before revealing myself."

"Makes sense," Caden said. Tension was building between her eyes, and she massaged there with two fingers. "So this isn't the best way to get back in?"

"Might be," Nuna said with a shrug. "We need to wait until it's clear of the guards. I'm supposed to meet the others fairly soon."

"Right, so more waiting," Caden said, and Henri grunted.

Chapter 8

C ate put her shoulders back and head up as she walked through a crowd of Uppers hoping to blend in. As she made her way down the hall, she searched for anything that might lead to either the other Underlings or someone from Undercity she could trust. She had no idea who was left alive among the people she used to live with before the tower. Some of them managed to make it across, but there were a few who she never saw again.

The market was in full swing with hawkers plying goods on various consumers who either paused to listen or pushed them aside. Evidently they still had enough Underlings left to keep supplies up.

"What kind of cloth is this?" exclaimed a disgruntled Upper as she tested the quality of a brown plaid dress with her fingers. "This is all patched and worn. You expect me to pay you credits for such garbage?"

The market man bowed his narrow head and took the dress from the rack.

"So sorry, my Upperlord. This should have never been put on display." He tossed the cloth at a small boy with dirty blond hair hovering near the counter.

"Cratchen, get rid of this. You got no eyes, boy? Put out merchandise like this again and I'll make certain you never see again." The scum turned back to the lady.

"Please, come this way. There are much better items on this rack."

The Upper peered down her nose at him. "Please, indeed. I have no interest in your substandard rags." Despite his protests and grovelling, she turned away, taking her young daughter with her.

"Honestly, I don't understand what's happened, but the quality of the market dropped in the last few months."

Her daughter assumed the same disgusted demeanour as her mother, and they disappeared in the crowd.

The marketer glared as she left, but morphed his face into a pleasant expression as a new customer stepped up.

Cate continued weaving through the crowd to the back halls between the stalls where the more important Uppers did not go.

"Hey, what are you doing back here?" It was the pasty boy from the clothing stall. He clutched a jelly sandwich in one dirty hand and a dribble of purple ran down his chin. "No customers behind the box."

"Oh, shut it, kid," Cate said as she strode past him. "I'm searching for someone."

"Who?" he asked while falling into step beside her, his green eyes bright and big.

She turned to the right past a decaying display of stuffed animals. "No one you know. Go away."

"I could help you find whoever it is."

"No, you can't. Don't you need to be somewhere else?"

"Nope. Shift's over. My time is all yours." He winked at her. "All yours."

Cate paused, trying to decide whether to go past the bizarre collection of headless human statues or the stall with the colourful plastic bobbles.

"Sorry, kid. You're a little young for me." She patted him on the head. "A little short too. Got other things to do, so go find someone else to flirt with."

The boy tugged on her skirt. "Aw, come on. Let me go with you. I promise not to flirt."

As she whirled around, she slapped his hand away. "Look, kid...."

"I can tell you're not an Upper."

A smart remark waited on her lips, but she glared at him instead. The underling was a scrawny creature in baggy pants and a t-shirt so big on him the cloth hung more like a dress with long sleeves.

"What are you talking about?"

The boy leaned against a stand of miniature gnomes, his big, innocent eyes holding a glint of cunning.

"You get me."

"No, I don't," she said, passing him.

He caught up with her. "Sure you do."

Cate clenched her hands and resisted the urge to pull on the scarf hiding her missing eye. "And what makes you think I'm not an Upper?"

"Simple. You're cranky and conda... condy... condicent...."

"Condescending?"

"Yeah, that, but not stuck up."

"Huh?"

"You don't look through me or at me like I'm rat pee on your shoe."

She frowned at him though she understood what he meant. As she grabbed his shirt, she lifted him a few inches off the ground. "You tell anyone, kid, and...."

"And you'll make me wish I hadn't. I get it," he said in a tight voice. "This isn't comfortable. If I promise to keep your secret, will you put me down?"

Cate let go, and he fell to the ground. "Fine. Don't have much choice, do I?"

The boy was smart and chose not to grin. "Nope." He stuck out his hand with a solemn tilt of his chin. "Cratchen's the name. Underling of the finest quality."

Despite herself, she laughed and shook his sticky hand. "Cate." She wiped the jelly off on a nearby curtain.

A tall couple of merchants strode by with their arms filled with boxes. Cate turned her face toward the nearest display, and they moved on without giving her a glance. Quickly, she continued while the boy fell into step beside her.

"So, what are we searching for?"

"People."

His narrow nose wrinkled in distaste. "People? We left a bunch behind in the main market, what do you want more of those for?"

"Specific people. I'm searching for specific people."

"Oh, specific people. Well, that's easy."

"It is?"

"Sure," he said with an elaborate wave. "There are specific people all over the place—specific creepers, specific Uppers, and even specific Underlings. Any specific specifics you had in mind?"

"Oh, you're a funny one," she said as she entered a hall that brought them away from the market. "All right, how about specific people near a pharmacy or medical place? Got any of those?"

"Don't know what a pharmacy is, but there's this doctor who lingers around the store rooms where marketers keep excess merch. Not too many people go there, especially after markets close. Don't know if he has any specific people down there, but he might."

She sucked on her bottom lip and tapped her thumb against her chin as she contemplated her options.

"Yeah, if I wanted to hide people or a person, that might be a good place to do it. Let's go."

"Hey, if we get caught down here without good reason, the marketers won't be too nice to us," he said, following behind.

"That's where you come in," she said, with a pat to his shoulder. "You just tell them your employer sent you to get some merch."

"And how do I explain you?"

"Don't you know?" she asked with a sarcastic grin. "I'm the new seller girl for your stall. You're showing me where you keep stuff at the same time."

"Uh, huh. Not bad. Might work." The kid took on a jaunty expression, hooking his hands in his pockets and taking on a cool strut.

"How old are you, kid?" Cate asked, amused.

"How old is anyone?" Cratchen responded with a sage frown.

Cate choked back a laugh. "Well, I'm guessing you are about twelve maybe thirteen years. I'm also guessing you spent most of those years working these markets as the go-boy to several different marketers."

"Yeah, you might be right," he said with an impish grin.

He flicked on a handlight as the tunnel grew darker the further they went.

The cement floor slanted downward and a chill cut through her clothes. As they came to a set of stairs, she wrapped her arms around herself, missing the space and air of the outdoors. The worn steps were damp and slightly slippery, and she kept a hand on the wall to keep from falling.

"Must be fun lugging boxes up these. Just how far do we go?"

"Eh, you get used to it. Plus, there's a lift at the other end. Don't like it much down here. It's all closed in, but so is most of Uppercity. Some areas are more closed than others, though, and this is one of them. The storage units are off to the left of the bottom of the stairs."

"What's off to the right?" she asked, peering down the tunnel.

"Never been down there, but that's where the medical guy lingers with his creepers. The kid shivered, his small shoulders shaking. "Gives me nightmares thinking about what they might be doing. How about we go this other way. No specific people, but much more interesting stuff and a lot less death." He pointed to the left.

Cate didn't move. Was this the pharmacy or the other place the Uppers mentioned? The doctor's pit. That was it. "Well, if you are searching for the wounded, going where the doctor goes makes sense," she muttered to herself, dreading the idea of searching in there.

"Sorry, kid. We can part ways now, but I think I gotta go to the right."

Cratchen grabbed her arm, his hazel eyes so big they took up most of his face. "Seriously? Not a good idea, honest."

"I get it. Like I said, you don't have to come. Just lend me your handlight and you can go back to skimming off marketers."

The kid's head swivelled from one direction to the other, his throat knot bobbing. "I'm not scared. I'm not."

"Never thought you were," she said, trying to get him to relax so she could continue her search without worrying about him. Time was getting short, and she wanted to search the medic area before she had to get back to the others. "Not even for a second. I don't want to go down there either. If I had another choice, I'd take it, but I think that's where I've got to go. At least, if I search and find nothing, I can cross it off my list and keep going."

"Is this important?" he asked, peering up at her, his thick eyebrows scrunching upward.

"Yeah," she said after a short pause. "Afraid so."

The sides of his mouth turned down and his eyes narrowed. "Then I go with you."

This kid didn't seem to know when to quit. "Why? You have no interest in this. You don't even know me and don't tell me it's because I'm the most beautiful girl you've ever seen. Romantic, mushy words don't sway me, and you're too young for me to find it anything other than creepy."

"Can't say," Cratchen said, his gaze becoming hooded. "You're doing something, something interesting. I've been wandering around this place with all these Uppers, marketers, and Underlings, and nothing changes. Nothing. But you seem to be doing things, and I want to too."

As she pondered his words and serious gaze, she felt like she was staring at herself. "You want to do something, huh? And you think I'm doing something interesting. That's a lousy excuse to follow me into who knows what kind of trouble, but I get it. Come on."

"Where are we going?" Jemma asked as Caden eased the door open just enough to peek outside.

She stretched out on the floor and peered through the crack while Henri stood over her, ready to take care of anyone who noticed them.

"Seems clear as far as I can tell. Wait, someone's coming. Yeah, it's a guard," she said as she pulled back, and Henri closed the door though he kept a hold on the knob.

"Maybe he'll keep going," Jemma said while she and Nuna waited behind the door.

Henri put his ear against the door, listening. "Footsteps," he whispered and motioned to Caden to back up with his free hand.

A cramp ran through her calf as she got up from the floor and moved beside the other two. Despite the pain, she tensed, waiting to help Henri.

Seconds later, the brute threw open the door and grabbed the guard as he went by. He tossed the brute guard across the room, and the guy hit the counter under the broken window with such force he nearly fell out of the room. Henri was on him before he could get up. He slammed his fist into the brute's face several times, and Caden heard the crunch of his nose breaking. She didn't know if he was unconscious or dead, but whatever he was Henri didn't seem to care as he flipped him out the window.

"And I will never say you make a lousy brute again," Caden said, staring out the window at the inert body lying in the grass. She blinked and stepped back as his hand jerked. "He's not dead."

"Of course not," Henri said with an indignant pout. "Not hurt that much."

"Well, much as I'd like to hang around admiring your handiwork, Henri, I doubt he's the only guard," Nuna said, standing by the door. "We should get out while we can."

"Wait, we can't just leave him there," Jemma said as she put her hands to her hips and studied him.

"Why not?" Henri asked. "He come around soon."

"That's just it. He'll regain consciousness soon enough and let all his other muscle friends know someone's back."

"So, what do we do?" Caden asked.

"Tie him up, at least," Jemma said, removing the scarf from her head. She hopped over the cupboard and proceeded to wrestle the unconscious brute about. "Come help me, Henri. We need to secure his hands behind his back. Caden, can you please see if you can find something to tie his legs together?"

While Henri climbed outside, Caden scanned the room, but aside from some furniture and a few cushions, there wasn't much to help them. She grabbed one of the panels of a curtain and tore a strip off long enough to use. Careful of the broken glass scattered about, she passed the pieces of cloth to Henri. After he and Jemma had finished securing the brute, they came back inside and everyone gathered by the door. The hall was clear for the moment, so, one by one, they snuck into the passage.

"I think the lock broke," Jemma said as she closed and pressed on the strip of plastic tape surrounding the frame, resealing the door.

"Well, let's make ourselves scarce before someone else comes around. The more distance we can put between us and this room, the better," Nuna said as they slipped down the hall. "I need to meet the others soon."

"Where?" Caden asked as she cast an eye around the inner areas of Uppercity. There weren't too many people around, but those who were wore an air she wouldn't ever be able to pretend to possess.

"There is a square not far from here, and one of the halls that shoot off from it leads to an abandoned scrounger tunnel." Nuna said, walking forward as though she belonged.

"Don't like this place," Henri said, looking uncomfortable. "Don't fit in."

"Just pretend you're in my service," Nuna advised, and Jemma raised an eyebrow at her.

"In your service?" The woman laughed under her breath, winking at her partner.

The colour rose in the other woman's cheeks. "Don't flirt. I'm still not sure I've forgiven you and your lost adventure."

Jemma smiled softly as Nuna linked her fingers in hers. They walked on in silence, and Caden suspected that forgiveness and reconciliation were much closer than Nuna portrayed.

Caden glanced sideways at Henri. Being that attached to someone did have attractive qualities, but what did love feel like? She barely understood liking and trusting. Yes, she cared for her family. At least, she had no desire to lose any of them or let them suffer in any way. She trusted them too, to the best of her ability, but was that love?

Henri glanced her way, and she dropped her gaze, her cheeks heating up.

"This way," Nuna said as they turned down another hall and entered a wide space with a platform at one end. Several different passages branched off in different directions.

"That hallway there leads to a stairwell where we think your other people might be," Nuna told them and pointed toward a passageway far on the other side of the square by the platform. "Quick, now," she said as she ducked down a hall leading in the opposite direction.

They hurried after her as Nuna stepped up her pace. As they passed door after door, Caden hoped they reached their hiding place soon. When they went past one apartment, a short, rounded, grey woman was screeching at a dowdy balding man with a full curly beard.

"It's gone. They're both gone. My shoes too."

"Yes, dear. My clothes are missing too, and some food, but the door was unlocked."

"Are you saying it's my fault?" she yelled, her voice going up two registers.

"No, no, dear," he insisted but was too late as she stormed out her door and straight into Henri.

"Get out of my way," she ordered, thwacking his chest.

Henri stared at her as though she was a weird sort of bug.

The Upperlord's sparse grey hair came loose from its pins as she caught sight of Nuna. Bright red rose on her face right to her roots and her pale eyes bugged out.

"You! That's my dress! How dare you?"

Nuna drew herself up as Toro snarled at the irate woman. "Your dress? I just purchased this dress yesterday. How dare you accuse me of stealing?"

"Oh, she doesn't mean..." her husband began before she shoved him aside.

"Yes, I do mean. Bought it yesterday, and I'm supposed to believe you?"

Taking on an imperious air, Nuna gestured to Henri. "Brute. This woman is not only accusing me of being a thief, she is in my way. Please remove her and her husband from my path."

Much to Henri's credit, he didn't give her away with a dopy, confused expression. Instead, he went stone-faced and stepped toward the couple.

"Come on, dear," her husband said with a gulp as he pulled her back toward their apartment. "I'm certain this is all a misunderstanding."

"But, but he promised me it was one of a kind. I only buy one of a kind," she babbled on, staring as though the greatest tragedy in life had struck her.

"We'll sort it out, I promise," her husband soothed as they closed their door.

Nuna traded a glance with the others and shrugged, a smirk on her lips. "We needed the clothes."

With a soft smile and a chuckle, Jemma linked her arm with Nuna's. "Ah, I missed you."

"Huh. Well, let's get going before anyone else makes a scene," Nuna said though she covered her spouse's hand with her own and held on.

They continued down the hall and went through a door tucked away from all the others.

"Jolon," Caden exclaimed as she caught sight of him leaning against the cement brick wall. Relieved, she hugged her brother tightly. "Thought I might never see you again. You're okay?" she asked, examining him. "Fancy clothes. I think I know where crabby woman's husband's wardrobe went."

"Huh?" he said, glancing down at his pants. "Oh. Yeah, grey lady with the balding husband? I ended up behind them on my way back here to meet Cate. They complained about everything and everyone as they went. Ducked quick when I realized which apartment belonged to them. Glad to see you're okay. Hi, Henri."

The brute grunted and fidgeted before wrapping him in a huge embrace. "You good. You okay." He snuffled, and Jolon gasped.

"Hey, let go. Need air," he grunted, whacking him in the arms until he moved away. "Missed you too," he said, coughing.

"So, where is Cate?" Caden asked as they proceeded down another hall to a dingy room that stunk of mould and urine.

"Haven't seen her yet. Just got here a few minutes ago myself." he said as he curled up in a corner. "Hey, Cad, you have something to eat? I've been waiting in a cold stairwell all day, and nothing even happened. Nearly drifted off a few times, so I thought I'd better get back here before I fell asleep and rolled down the stairs. If Dorkas went down there to get rid of anyone from the tower, he didn't bring them out that way."

He scrubbed his face with trembling hands. "I just can't get them out of my head."

"Yeah. We'll find them. We will." She dug in her stash and handed him a plastic dish with fish and rice leftovers in it. "Here. It's good."

Sceptical, he sniffed the food before scooping some up and putting it in his mouth. "Mhhhmm."

Jemma handed another container to Nuna. "You'll love this."

"Who are you?" Jolon asked, spitting food particles with every word.

"This is Jemma," Caden said while Nuna ate. "She's Nuna's spouse."

Her brother's eyebrows drew together in confusion. "I thought—ah, never mind," he said, going back to his food.

Caden scanned the room. It was small and dank with no light and the insipid fragrance of wet brick. "How did you guys find this place?"

"We took a shortcut," Jolon said between mouthfuls. "This is good. What is it?"

"Fish," Jemma said as she tried to find a clean place to sit.

Jolon choked. "As in Mrs. Fish?"

Caden kicked him in the leg. "No, dopy. As in creatures that swim in clean, clear water."

He pondered his food for a moment before shovelling more in his mouth.

"So, what do we do now?" Caden asked as she moved back toward the door. The place was so dark, and she longed for the light. "I don't want to stay here if we don't need to."

"We are waiting for Cate," Nuna said, putting her empty container aside. "She should show up soon unless she ran into trouble."

"What kind of trouble?" Caden asked, not liking the sound of that.

"Hard to say. I don't know much about your Uppercity, but it's not a pleasant place. Many of your Uppers possess an overinflated idea of their self worth."

"Figures," Caden muttered a bitter flavor in her mouth.

"Did you discover anything useful at all?" Nuna asked, turning to Jolon.

He pushed his plastic container away and wrapped his arms around his legs. "I found out that most brutes can stand still for a long time. They're like statues, immovable statues. Dorkas never came back, so I don't know what happened to him, but after about five hours I heard some people descending from on high, so I had to get out of there. Plus, my ass was cold, and my stomach empty. I ate all the food I took from grey lady's place, but it only lasted so long."

Nuna pursed her lips and began to pace, rubbing her arms thoughtfully.

Caden slipped out of the room and leaned against the stone wall, her head ringing. She closed her eyes and massaged her temples, wishing she could lie down.

"You okay?" Henri asked, appearing beside her.

Irritated, she opened one eye and frowned. Of course, he would follow her. He made a terrific shadow. "Body's sore. Joints hurt. Head throbbing. Otherwise, I'm fine. How about you?" she asked before her legs betrayed her and she slumped to the ground. His voice faded away, and she embraced the silence that followed.

Chapter 9

"What now?" Cratchen asked, tugging at Cate's shirt as she crouched outside a grimy wooden door.

"Quiet," she said, swatting his hand. "I'm listening to see if anyone's in there."

"No one's in there. At least, no one living."

She glared down at him. "And how do you know that?"

The kid twitched his shoulders in a careless shrug. "I always watch who comes and goes. Storage rooms make perfect hiding places when you don't want anyone to find you."

"Makes sense," she decided and gave a hard tug on the handle, the door slid sideways on its track, rattling noisily.

As she went inside, she shone Cratchen's handlight around the room. The place stank like death and rot. She held her breath and tucked her nose under her t-shirt. The kid hung back near the door, his face pale.

Teeth clenched, she took hesitant steps forward. The dark made it difficult to see what was around her, but the room didn't seem too large. The light glanced off steel cupboard doors and several narrow metal beds on wheels. Tarps covered most of the beds. A few were lumpy, and she dreaded the idea of searching under the fabric to see what was hiding there. All the moisture left her mouth as she held her breath and flipped back the cloth on the nearest one.

Bile rushed up from her gut at the sight of the decayed face, which was almost unrecognizable as human, but had way too much hair to be

Mr. Peterson. Stomach churning, she moved to the next one. The thudding of her heart reverberated through her body. Terrified, she tried to lift the next covering, but her arms were like lead.

Something rustled behind her. She whirled about. "Kid?" she said, her voice raising several octaves.

"Wasn't me," he said by her blind side his voice tight. Eyes wide, he backed toward the tunnel. "Let's go."

Despite her fears, she ignored him, inching toward the sound, her light moving over the area. Someone was there hunched in the corner. She moved closer, every nerve in her body ready to bolt.

The person coughed, his stringy hair moving away from his face.

"Pa?" she gasped and rushed to him. "Uh, Mr. Peterson?" Carefully, she brushed his hair further from his face, shining the light on him. He raised a limp hand and squinted. His face was two shades lighter than pale. Dark stains of blood, body fluids, and grime covered his shirt and pants.

Cate put the handlight on the floor, letting it shine upward. "You okay?" she asked as she took his face in her hands. "Peterson? Pa? Hey."

"That your specific person?" the kid asked as he edged toward them. He held his shirt over his face.

"Yeah, that's him. We gotta get him out of here." She grabbed his arm and draped it over her shoulder, pulling him up from the floor. He groaned and coughed, but made no effort to stop her.

"We?" Cratchen said, and she glared at him. "Hey, I don't owe you anything, and lugging near dead bodies through the market is not my idea of a good idea."

"I thought you wanted to do something different. Well, this is different. Or are you a lot of talk and no substance?"

The kid shifted from foot to foot before turning away. "Wait here."

"Perfect," she muttered as he disappeared. Was he coming back to help or did he run to tell someone she was there? Whatever he was doing, she wasn't keen on waiting to find out. After propping Mr. Peterson in a broken metal chair, she picked up the handlight and stuck it under her arm, light forward so she could see.

"Okay, let's get out of here." Muscles straining, she hauled him back onto his feet. The man's head lolled back as his breathing turned raspy. Slowly, she dragged him toward the opening but froze as she heard a rumbling coming toward her. Anxious, she peered around the edge of the wall and saw a huge plastic bin rolling their way.

"Not the most comfortable ride, but he'll never make it if we carry him," the kid said, peeking his head around the back of the bin.

"What am I supposed to do? Dump him inside?" she asked, staring at the high edges.

"Yeah, I packed a bunch of clothes and blankets, and stuff in the bottom to make it more comfortable."

The kid rushed over to the other side of Mr. Peterson and helped her lift his near dead weight into the cart. The wounded man moaned as he tumbled inside, legs and arms twisted about.

Huffing, Cate rested a moment against the side. "How are we supposed to get this up the stairs, brilliant boy?"

"Like I said before, there's a lift at the end of the storage hall," he told her with an impish grin.

A laugh broke from her despite the exhaustion and fear pulling at her. "Right. Brilliant."

"We better go, though," he said as he piled more material on Mr. Peterson. "The stores will be closing soon, and marketers will come down here to replenish supplies."

After several deep breaths, she pushed the cart, and it rattled as they went down the passageway. Lanterns hung from metal pegs between the storage doors on this side of the hall. They paused at one stall, and Cratchen piled a bunch of clothes onto Mr. Peterson. When they got to the lift, the kid nodded to a lanky guy sitting on a wooden chair by a long row of ropes connected to metal gears rigged to the floor and ceiling.

"Hey, Dobbs. Just bringing a load up."

Dobbs nodded, a toothless smile hiding under his hooked nose and full olive cheeks. "Up and down. That's the day of it, eh?" He helped them shove the cart on the wooden platform.

"Yep." Cratchen tossed him a casual, two-finger salute. "See you later."

The man's head shook while he hauled on the ropes. Slowly, he disappeared as they went up through the opening to the second floor, the wood and gears creaking. The light grew as they left the storage area behind. People milled about, closing their stalls and gathering to share the day. They pushed the cart off the lift and wove through the crowd.

"We should have waited until everyone left the market," Cate said, feeling inconspicuous.

"This place takes hours to empty out. I don't think specific person has that much time."

Cate had to admit he was probably right. She kept on pushing, and they came to the hall leading to the square.

A large brute with patchy skin and a pug nose stepped in front of their cart. "Where you think you going?"

"Got a delivery," the kid said with a polite nod. "Big order due tonight. Cranky Upper waiting."

The brute peered down the narrow ridge of his warped nose and into the cart. Cate held her breath and went over the various ways she might be able to take him down. Any options were limited by his extensive array of muscles and the narrowness of the hallway. Plus, the only weapon available was a hanger from the cart. She doubted it would do much damage though a swift poke in the eye might work.

Cratchen fidgeted as though impatient and put on a fear-filled expression. "Come on. Please, you gotta let me through. I've caught the stick twice today. If I don't get this order delivered, my boss will lock me in the storage room without supper again."

The brute's beady eyes narrowed as he stepped aside. "Get going before I use stick too."

Cratchen grovelled and bowed as they rolled the cart by him. Cate kept her head down, knowing how brutes could be. A meaty hand caught her arm, and she cursed inside.

"You stay with me," the brute said, leaning in close his grin lecherous.

"Ah, she's part of the delivery," Cratchen said with a wink. "Pure goods hand chosen. You could take her if you want, but the client ain't gonna be too happy if she shows up spoiled."

His lips curled up as though he had a right to be annoyed, and Cate wished she had a metal pipe to use on his more sensitive parts. The brute let go, and they continued, leaving the creep behind.

"I guess I should say thanks for saving me from making him eat one of the hangers," she muttered as they went.

"Ah, his kind of creep is easy to get around. All ya need to do is push a little fear his way, and he'll fold," the kid said, his chest puffed up.

Cate hid a smile behind a scowl. He wasn't too bad, her kind of resourceful Underling. "Turn here," she said as they reached the hall, which led to the scrounger tunnel. "I got it from here if you want to take off."

"Hey, I've gone this far," he protested as he scrubbed his head. "Besides, I gotta bring all this stuff and the cart back, or I'll catch it."

As she glanced behind them, she chewed on her lip as she decided what to do. "Yeah, well, if you hang with me, you'll definitely catch it."

"If I'm gonna get into trouble either way, at least with you it will be interesting along the way."

"Ah, huh, you think so, do you?"

"Yep."

"Fine, then get the door," she said, poking her chin toward the entrance to the passage. Whether the others were back or not, she had no idea, but she had to get Mr. Peterson out of sight.

The cart clanked and banged as they pulled and pushed it through the doorway.

"Shh, or we'll draw a crowd," she said under her breath, glancing every which way for people. Aside from a couple of stragglers in the square, who threw a few of glares, no one else was around.

"Hey, I'm not the only one driving this thing," he said, cursing as they gave one last push and the cart went through, almost running him over in the process. He stumbled and fell, but picked himself up with a quick hop.

"Perfect," he grumbled as he dusted off his palms.

"What's wrong?" she asked as the area became dark with the closing of the door. Cate pulled out the handlight and examined his hand. "Eh, just a couple of scratches. You'll live."

"Stings," he muttered but tugged on the cart. "Never been back here before. Where to now?"

"Not far. There's a room just ahead where the others should be."

Cratchen's bug-eyes narrowed as his body tensed. "Others? What others?"

"Relax. No one's going to eat you. They're family to him and friends to me."

"Sure," he said though doubt lingered in his expression. "Makes sense, I... yipe!"

With a squeal, he ducked behind the cart as Nuna's dog charged down the passage, barking and yapping.

"Hey," Cate said as the animal jumped at her. "Calm down, mutt." He put his paws on the top of her thighs and yelped again, his tongue rolling to one side of his open mouth.

"Family too?" the kid asked as though being smart would bring back his courage.

"Funny, no. This is Toro," she said, scratching the dog behind the ears.

"Don't worry; he won't hurt you," Nuna said as she joined them.

"Hi," Cratchen said, staring. "You're quiet."

"And you two are loud. Got poor Toro all riled up," she said, eyeing the kid. "You picked up another stray?"

"Yeah, and someone else," Cate said, pulling back the clothes from Mr. Peterson. "He's hurt. Pretty bad as far as I can tell."

"Ohh," she gasped, her hands going to the injured man. "He's got a pulse, but it's very weak. We've got to get him somewhere safe."

"Yeah, but how? Where?" Cate asked, pacing. "This place is too cold and damp to keep him here, and we don't have any good resources to help. Don't even have much water."

Nuna gestured down the tunnel with her head. "Come on. We've found some stragglers who can help."

They entered the room, pushing the cart ahead of them. Despite the darkness, Cate recognized the bulk of Henri bent over someone in one of the corners.

"I'm all right," barked a voice she knew well.

"Caden?" she called and rushed over to her. "You okay?"

"Fine. I'm fine. I got too tired," Caden said with a glare, though her complexion was like dull stone, a slight flush darkened her cheeks. "That's all," she protested, pushing Cate's hands away. "Don't get all worried. Where have you been?"

"Nice change of subject," Cate said as she sat back. "I was hunting around the market." A lump stuck in her throat, making her hesitate before adding, "I found your pa."

Caden's face lit up, and she struggled to stand, but Henri wouldn't let her.

"What? Get out of my way, brute. Where is he?"

"Calm down," Cate said, leaning back on her haunches. "He's there in the cart, but he's wounded, and we need to get some help."

"So, what we do?" Henri asked as Caden slapped at his hands.

"You let me get up, for starters."

"No, he's right; you shouldn't get up," Nuna said.

"We should take them both back to the house," said a voice Cate didn't recognize.

She turned slightly to get the woman out of her blind side. "Who are you?"

"Oh, this is Jemma," Nuna said, putting a hand on the other woman's arm. "She's with me. Jemma, this is Cate and...." She paused, gesturing to the kid.

"Cratchen," Cate said, nodding warily to the newcomer. "More people. Perfect. Just what we need."

"Jemma's right. We need to get back to the house where they'll be safe," Nuna said, leaning over the cart.

"Hey, I got some water," Jolon exclaimed as he burst in the room. "What? Oh, Cate. What you find?" He turned to the kid. "Who's he?"

"She found your father," Nuna said, taking the jug from him.

"What? Where?" He twisted about, searching the room.

Nuna put a hand on his shoulder and guided him to the cart. "He's here. Alive, but not well."

"Pa?" he called, pushing more of the clothes to the side. "Pa? You okay?" His voice quivered with worry and fear.

"Don't worry, we're going to help him, Jolon, he's going to be fine," Nuna said, squeezing his shoulder.

"We go," Henri said as he scooped Caden off the floor despite her protests. "Get mad at me all want. Don't care. We go and hurry. Jol, you and others all push cart. We go." With that, he strode out of the room.

"Guess we go," Cate said to the kid, and he shrugged.

"Guess so." He tilted his head, his face curious. "Where do we go?"

She arched an eyebrow. "Don't have a clue. You sure you still want to go with me?"

The kid's grin grew from ear to ear. "Why not? We go."

"We go," she repeated and laughed.

Teddy got up from the couch and gingerly put some weight on his foot.

"Don't do that," Deb advised as she came in with a pile of books. "Ma said if you want to damage that foot for good then go ahead and walk. If you want it to get better, stay the hell off it."

He chuckled and sat back down. "Somehow I think she muttered that under her breath."

The little girl shrugged a shoulder and dumped the books on the couch. "Kinda. Found these in the room by the kitchen. Ma said you might like them, and that wasn't under her breath."

"Let's see what you found." He picked up a softcover book and flipped through the pages. Night was full on, and he put the book aside to light a few more candles.

"How's Georges?"

Deb grabbed a book and curled up in a chair by the fire, pulling a blanket over her. "Ummm. I think she's doing better. Ma's with her," she answered, her attention on her book.

"What's that?" he said as he heard a ruckus outside.

"Huh?" His sister glanced up from her story, blinking.

Something outside crashed again, and Teddy leaped to his feet. "Ahhhgh," he yelped as his ankle gave way, and he fell back on the couch.

"Good idea," Deb said as she got up. "Let me check."

"Deb, wait." He tried to grab her, but she squirmed away.

"Who's there?" she sang and skipped up to the entrance.

"Deb!" he shouted but was too late.

She opened the door and squealed, running outside.

"Deb? Deb!" he called, hopping around the couch and limping toward the exit.

"Can't leave you alone for a second," Cate said as she came in.

Stunned, he stared at her, breathing heavy. For the last couple of days, he pictured finding her safe, and he had so many words, compliments, to give. Now, as she appeared before him, all his practiced phrases failed him.

"You're in a dress," he managed and shut his mouth, hoping not to say anything else rediculous.

She made a face and leaned against the back of a chair. "Smooth."

Henri strode in behind her with Caden in his arms.

"Stop," she ordered, frustration plain on her face. "Teddy, make him stop."

The brute rushed over to the couch and put her down. "Stay."

His sister pushed her hair out of her face. "You stay."

"Caden!" Deb shouted as she ran in with Toro by her side. With a great hop onto the couch and wrapped her in a hug. "Missed you."

"Missed you too," she said as they curled up together.

Henri rushed back out of the house while Teddy limped back to a chair.

"What happened?" he asked Caden but didn't hear her answer as Henri came back in with his father in his arms and Jolon, Nuna, and Jemma following behind.

"Ma? Ma!" shouted Jolon, rushing to the stairs.

"Bring him upstairs," Nuna ordered, escorting the brute.

"Jolon?" Ma called, appearing at the top. "Oh," she shouted rushing toward Henri. "Tru."

Nuna caught her. "He's still alive, but he's lost lots of blood, and I think his wound is infected."

Ma kicked into doctor mode. "Nuna, get some water boiling. Deb, there are some cotton towels in a drawer in the kitchen. Get me the lot. I need scissors too, a bowl and salt. There is some in the cupboard by the stove. Henri, follow me." She rushed away, and everyone else scrambled, leaving Teddy with Caden.

Breathless, Teddy sunk further into his chair. "You okay?" Teddy managed as he tried to put together his thoughts.

"Been better, been worse," she said, scrubbing at her face with her hands. "Think I'm in a bit of shock." She glanced toward him, her eyes red. "You're kind of pale yourself."

"Ahh, I, yeah, shock. That's, yeah." He grabbed a cushion and hugged it tight. "What happened?"

His sister sank back on the couch, tears running down her face. "Cate found him. He looks so bad."

Teddy was about to say something when he caught a glimpse of a small boy by the door. The new arrival waved and inched his way inside.

"Hi."

"Hi?" Teddy said, staring at the knobby, scrawny, pale child. "Who are you?"

Chapter 10

Cate rushed upstairs, her arms full of supplies. The place wasn't too big, and it was easy to find the bathroom by the sound of Mrs. Peterson's voice. Henri put Mr. Peterson in the tub, and Mrs. Peterson was in the process of cutting away his filthy clothing.

"The wound goes clear through, which is good, but it needs cleaning, and he's quite dehydrated. Need to get some liquids in him."

"Mrs. Peterson, I have the salt and couple of bowls," Cate said, putting them on the counter. "And Jemma said you might need this." She held up a clear cylinder with a rubber bulb on one end. "Not sure what for, but...."

"Here's water," Deb exclaimed, hopping in. A gasp escaped her as she stopped at the door, her face going so white she was almost see-through.

Her mother took the pail from her, handed it to Cate, and whirled the little girl around. "Go. Henri, take her downstairs and make sure she stays there."

The brute did as ordered and ushered Deb out of the room. Mrs. Peterson poured some of the water into the bowl and took one of the clothes. While she proceeded to wash her husband, Cate leaned against the counter, staring at the tiled grey floor, unsure of what to do.

"The baster was a good idea," Mrs. Peterson said though Cate wasn't sure she was talking to her. "I can use it to pressure wash the wound." Moisture glinted in her eyes as she paused and licked her thin lips. With a sniff, she rinsed the cloth. "Well, it will be better than nothing."

She passed the bowl and its filthy contents to Cate. "Get rid of this and keep the water coming. We'll need lots."

Jemma appeared in the door with another bowl and several purplish plants soaking in steaming water, which sent a soothing fragrance through the air. "I have found this little flower to be quite medicinal," she said as she handed the bowl to Mrs. Peterson. "It seems to work well as an antiseptic."

"Where did you find it?" Mrs. Peterson asked, examining the contents of the bowl. "Such a soothing scent."

"There is quite a bit growing in almost every backyard," Jemma said as she took another cloth and helped to clean Mr. Peterson.

Cate took the dirty bowl and left, feeling awkward and out of place. As she passed one of the bedrooms, she saw Nuna stripping one of the beds.

Exhausted, she went down the stairs and into the backyard. After she had dumped the bowl, she sat down on the wooden steps and stared at the overgrown trees and plants half-hidden by the night's shadows. The little purple flowers grew in bushes by the deck. She plucked a few and rubbed the tiny buds between her fingers, sniffing the sweet, aromatic fragrance.

"What's up?" Caden asked as she sat down beside her.

"Aren't you supposed to be resting?"

"Ugh, don't start." Caden rubbed a hand across her forehead. "I'm nervous and anxious, and don't want to lay there wondering."

Cate offered her a flowery stem. "Here. Sniff this. It helps. Peaceful... comforting."

Her friend's expression turned sceptical, but she took the plant. "Not bad," she said as she sniffed.

"Can I have some?" asked Deb in a small voice as she squeezed between them. "I'm anx... an... anxious too," she said, hiccupping her way through the word.

"Here." Cate handed her a twig, and Caden passed one to Henri as he sat down beside her.

Teddy hobbled out with the help of the kid, and they all sat in a row, sniffing flowers and staring at anything, but each other.

"I can't believe I'm outside," said Cratchen.

"Yeah, after years of dark, we're out in the open," Teddy said.

"It's still dark."

"Thanks, Cate, that's not what I meant."

"Just saying," she inhaled deeply, and silence fell again.

"Hey, Nuna decided we all should eat something. Oh, Jeeze, what's this?" Jolon asked as he came out with a tray of crackers and jam and saw them all lined up sniffing flowers.

"It's soothing," Caden said, plucking more flowers.

"So's food." He sat down beside them and passed the tray to Henri as the brute handed him a piece of flower. Sniffing it, he tilted his head and nodded. "Yeah, it is... it's nice."

A gentle breeze curled around them as they passed the tray around. The stars came out, and they waited.

"Teddy."

"Hummm."

"Teddy."

He whacked at the hand tugging at his arm.

"Hey, no hitting. Come on, hero. You can't sleep here. Besides, it's morning, anyway. Everyone else has wandered off to somewhere more comfortable, and I think Tanna, Jeana, Jemma or whatever her name is, is making some kind of weird goopy breakfast."

A kink in his neck sent a stab of pain through his shoulder. "Ah, hi, Cate," he said with a groan and a stretch.

"Yeah, that's what happens when you fall asleep leaning against a pole."

Working some moisture in his mouth, he yawned. "And here I thought the pain in my neck was you."

"Thanks, lots," she said, scowling as she helped him up. "Missed you too. How's the ankle?"

"Better, I think," he said and put a little pressure on his foot. "Doesn't hurt as much. Just feels stiff."

"Good. Come on before that kid eats the house. I gotta stop picking up stragglers."

Teddy followed her, pleased with the amount of mobility that had returned to his foot. Aside from a tight sensation brought on from lack of use, the limb felt almost normal again.

During the night, he and the others shared stories of their adventures since getting separated. All the details of the Upperlords and their actions made him so angry; he wanted to hurt them in ways he felt ashamed he had the ability to imagine. It cast a dark shadow of helplessness on every moment of his life.

"Ah, yes. This place is getting quite the crowd now," he said and perched on one of the painted blue kitchen chairs.

"The rest are in the living room. Don't you want to join them?" she asked, fidgeting with a flower-shaped plate on the table.

Strands of her copper hair curled around the curves of her face, and his fingers itched to brush them aside. All the while they were parted, he never noticed how much he missed her until she was with him again. Now, a tightness deep inside relaxed despite all the chaos surrounding them. He propped his leg on another chair and massaged his calf.

"Not really. How's my father?"

Fatigue clung to her as she sat down across from him, leaning her elbow against the table. "Sleeping. Your mother hasn't left his side all night. Georges is up and discussing the faults of the world with Jemma while Nuna is keeping an eye on your mother. Turns out Jemma's pretty handy with healing and plants, and stuff. They're an amazing group, actually, those women. Your father too, he's amazing too. You're lucky."

"You didn't sleep?"

"No," she said as she ran her fingers along the edge of one of the plates on the table. "Not much." She kept her gaze on the plate, twirling it about on the wood surface.

"What's up?"

"Not much," she said and crossed her arms, her attention far away.

"Not convinced."

With a sharp glance his way, she scowled as though annoyed. "Don't you want breakfast?"

For a moment, he wanted to break down her walls, but that would only push her farther away. He liked her, rough edges and all. The kiss he stole still lingered on his lips in the quiet moments when he was alone. But if she had feelings for him, so far she didn't let them show.

"Fine. Yeah, I'm hungry," he said at last, getting up from the table and limping into the living room.

Everyone was there now, except for Ma. Jolon shifted over for him on the couch while Nuna handed him a bowl and a spoon.

"This isn't bad," Jolon said as he scooped some of his meal up. "Hot, sweet. Pretty tasty, actually."

Teddy stirred the lumpy brown mush. He took a mouthful and found Jolon was right. "Thanks, Jemma."

"Yes, she's a pretty good cook," Georges said as she took another bowl.

"Good scrounger," Jemma corrected and sat by Nuna. "I've had a few years of exploring any house I could find for anything to eat. Much of what is left isn't any good, but some stuff in sealed packages and containers is useable. Don't know how good it is for a person, but it always fills the belly."

"You look like you're moving better, boy," Georges said while enjoying the food.

"You too," he replied between mouthfuls.

The Upperlord barked a laugh, which made her cough. "Almost. With the help of your mother I might live forever."

"I should bring some food up to Ma," Caden said, her eyes sunk into her head and her body hunched over like she was done supporting her.

"I take," Henri said, moving quickly before she could protest. Nuna passed him a bowl, and he disappeared up the stairs.

"How is he?" Teddy asked Caden as she sunk back into the couch, her face a mix of annoyance and gratitude.

"Better... comfortable... safe, at least," Nuna answered for her. "Though he still has a fever."

Jemma rose and took a pot off the stove. "Deb, you and the kid help clean up these dishes, please."

"If I had known I would become someone else's servant, I would have stayed at the market," Cratchen muttered as Deb shoved a bowl at him.

"We're little, which means we clean and get out of the room so they can talk." Deb's expression twisted into a frown stolen directly from Ma. "Let's go. At least, we can go out on the porch to wash the dishes. I like outside."

"Me too," he said with a sigh. "Guess that's a plus."

"Your father lost lots of blood," Nuna told him after they left. "He's dehydrated and weak. We're giving him as many fluids as we can, but it's hard to say if he'll make it. Sorry, Teddy. I just don't want to lie to you and pretend he'll be fine. He needs rest and quiet. We'll keep the wound clean as best as we can."

A heavy silence fell on the room. She placed a hand on Teddy's leg.

"Good thoughts, boy. He's here now with those who love him."

"He needs medicine."

Everyone turned toward Georges, who sat up and tapped her fingers on the table in front of her. "He needs medicine, and I think I know where to get some."

"Where?" Caden asked, leaning forward, attentive and serious.

"There's a storage room in the medical wing that is filled with all kinds of medication."

"The pharmacy," Cate said. "Your sister mentioned it. I wasn't certain what she was talking about, but I'm assuming that's what it is."

"Right," said Georges. "They have a working lab there too and the knowledge to make more. It's a skill that the family passed down through their generations. If there is anything to help him, it will be there."

Teddy rubbed at his dry eyes, anger writhing under the surface at the idea of the Uppers keeping such medicine to themselves. "I don't understand this. I mean, we all knew there was a doctor, and... and that he had access to some medicine, but a whole lab full of stuff? A whole setup that could have healed..." He stumbled in his thoughts as his emotions rose. "What kind of elitism... what kind of privilege?" His words caught in his throat. He paused and took several deep breaths.

"Did you know, Georges?" he asked a little more sharply than he intended as he fought to control his anger. "Did you know what your sister and her friends were like in the core? That they would dispose of more than a hundred people because they are an inconvenience or a threat to their lifestyle?"

Georges rested back, meeting his gaze. "No. Contrary to what you might think, Belinda hid much of what she did from me. I knew she was mean, conniving, and selfish, but I never thought she would go as far as she has."

"But you know about the medicine, the pharmacy, " Cate said, her posture tense like a cat wanting to rip apart its prey.

"Yes," the woman said with a slow nod. "I did, I do. Though there wasn't much I could do with that information. The area is heavily guarded and difficult to get to. My position was precarious, and I would have been the first suspect if anything went missing. Not that that really mattered to me. I did manage to get through a few specialty items. Your mother got most of them though I believe your father honoured my wishes and didn't tell anyone where he got them from."

"Fair enough," Cate said after a moment and she traded a glance with Teddy. "Guess that means some of us need to go shopping."

"Yeah, well, I'm not staying behind for this one."

"Your foot," Jolon protested, but Teddy shook his head.

"Is fine. At least, it's fine enough for me to walk on. Besides, I'm the best reader here, and we have to make sure we get the right medication. Plus, we still need to find Mrs. Fish and the rest of our crowd. I'm hoping we're not too late."

"I'm going too," Caden said, jumping to her feet.

"No, you're not," Teddy, Cate, and Nuna said together.

"I can't stop the boy from going," Nuna told her with a firm voice. "He's not so bad off, and he's right about the reading, but you, you've done too much. You need rest."

"Henri can come with us," Teddy said, avoiding Nuna's sharp, disapproving gaze.

"And I'll go too," Jolon said, with a dramatic sigh. "Might as well volunteer before you volunteer me."

"Go where?" Deb asked as she came in with Cratchen in tow.

"Nowhere you need to be concerned about," Caden said. "Now you two find something else to do."

The little girl slumped as though melting. "Aww, come on. We'll be good and quiet."

"We're going back to the Uppercity to find some medicine for Pa," Teddy told her, ignoring Caden's glare. "And, no, you can't come. I need you here to care for Cad and make sure she doesn't come searching for us," he added with a smirk.

"Ha, ha," Caden responded and stuck her tongue out at him.

"I'd go, but I don't really want to go back to the dark," Cratchen said with a hint of fear in his eyes.

"Course you're not going," Deb said with a possessive turn of her chin. "You're my friend now, and you're staying with me."

Cate laughed. "Sorry, kid. You're in for it now."

He shrugged and grinned. "Only if I want to be. Haven't had a friend in a long time. Might be a good change."

Deb wriggled her eyebrows in her most Ma serious expression.

"Then again, I might just go for an adventure," the kid said with a wary glance Deb's way.

"Ugh, come on. Let's pick more of those flowers," Deb said though she chuckled. She grabbed his arm and dragged him out of the room.

"Poor kid," Georges said, snickering.

"Somehow I think he can keep up," Cate said. "I doubt he does anything he doesn't want to. All right. When do we leave?"

"We don't know where we're going yet," Teddy said, turning to Georges. "Can you draw us a map?"

"I'll go collect some supplies," Jolon said with a resigned slouch as though the job was a torture he expected.

"I'll help you," Nuna offered and followed him into the kitchen.

Cate slapped her hands against her lap as she got up. "Guess I'll find some paper and something to draw with."

After they had left, Georges laced her fingers behind her head and tapped her fingers on her scalp.

"Interesting bunch of people you've collected."

"I like them."

"It's a good thing, or this whole journey will be for nothing. You sure you can do this with your wounded foot and all?"

He pressed his foot to the floor, checking it. It ached but held his weight. "I'll manage."

"Bring some kind of cane. It will reduce the strain and make a handy weapon if the need arises."

"How dangerous and how hard will it be getting into the medical stores?" Teddy asked, doubts twinging.

The Upperlord pursed her lips thoughtfully before she answered. "Quite. They have the best brutes covering the entrance and the place is locked tight when no one is inside."

"I'm pretty good with locks," Cate said as she came back with some paper and a pencil, which she handed to Georges. "My depth perception might not be so good, but I can almost see with my fingers."

"Nifty skill," Georges observed, leaning over the coffee table and putting pencil to paper. "This is all by memory so, I can't absolutely guarantee the accuracy of this map, but it will give you a guide. Usually, the guards change every three hours throughout the day. The potion-makers are a serious bunch. Unlike the doctor or other Upperlords, they start work early in the morning and don't finish until late in the night.

I figure your best way in is during the night shift. They get hungry after a while, and if you can intercept their meal delivery, you could take their place and slip in. Once inside, one of you will have to create a diversion while the others grab the supplies. Now, here's a list of what you want to get. Any bottle marked antibiotics is good, plus they have bags of saline fluid as well as blood they keep in a fridge. You'll want the bags with an 'o' on them."

"They keep bags of blood?" Cate said with a disgusted expression.

"Yes," she said gravely. "You'll also want to grab a couple of IVs. That is a clear plastic hose and a needle that looks like this." She sketched out a picture. "I would grab whatever else you can while you're there. Bandages and such will be handy." The former Upperlord paused, fidgeting with the pencil before she continued to write.

"If you can find some, pick up some ACE Inhibitors, Aldosterone Inhibitor, Beta-Blockers, Potassium, and Magnesium. And aspirin, though that one tends to be difficult to find."

"What are they for?" he asked as she handed him the list.

As she leaned back in her chair, she drew a measured breath, her face losing all depth of colour. "My heart. It's a weak, unreliable muscle that tends to complain these days."

"Got it," Teddy said, folding the paper and putting it in his pocket. "We'll do our best."

"How come they have all this?" Cate asked, holding her hands wide. "We found working fridges and lots of supplies no one else has had for a long time."

"Uppercity has always had far more than they ever let any Underling suspect. When the meteor destroyed most of everything, and society fell apart, a few families managed to protect a portion of what was left of the domes. Part of this included a thermoelectric station that got its power via volcanic heat deep underground. A portion of the system was damaged, but they managed to get it working well enough to provide power to a segment of the remaining city. This is what became Uppercity. However, the power was relatively unreliable at first, and they feared sharing it."

"Why?"

She pulled her hair back and stretched wearily. "Oh, because they thought if they did it might fail and then no one would have anything. They said they would only keep it from the rest of the survivors until society rebuilt itself and they established stability, but greed took over."

"And they kept everything for themselves no matter what it meant to the rest of the people," Cate said with disgust.

"Pretty much. Well, I will go upstairs and send your brute down. I'm tired now and need to sleep." She paused at the foot of the stairs and turned back. "Good luck. Keep safe."

"Thanks," Teddy said as she left. As he leaned back, he gave a low, dry chuckle and fiddled with the pencil. "I only ever wanted to find peace." He chuckled. "Sounds corny and simple, but it's true. I always pictured opening a good school and helping society put itself back together—people healthy and thriving, living outside, having families. I always wanted things good so I could write stories and be with my family."

"At least, you wanted something," Cate said as she sank into the chair opposite him.

Teddy glanced at her. "Don't you?"

"I guess," she said, her fingers playing with the arm of the chair. "Not really. I only ever wanted to be safe with a space of my own."

"I'm sorry."

"What for?" she asked, a fire sparking in her eye. Colour brightened her cheeks, and she donned a defensive tilt to her chin.

His pulse quickened as he found himself contemplating the curve of her lips. The urge to kiss her came over him again. Confused, he rubbed his hands along his thighs.

"Ah, I pushed you out of your space back in the tower. If I had respected you, you would probably be safe right now."

At his words, her posture relaxed. "You've apologized for that before."

"Yes, but I've realized a new level of wrong in what I did, and that deserves another apology. If I respected you and your home...you would be safe right now."

Licking her lips, she studied him. "Yeah, well, maybe, maybe not. Besides, I'd miss all the fun of witnessing you stumble around trying to be amazing. And that would be..."

"Horrible?" he offered, and she grinned, an inviting smile that drew him to her.

"Yeah, horrible."

"I don't try to be amazing," he objected though he didn't mind the way she said it. Without thinking, he brushed his fingers against her hand.

"Of course, you do," she said and returned his touch. "You're the type. You see a problem, and you want to make it all better. I get it."

"Got your stashes," Jolon said as he came back.

As quick as they could, he and Cate pulled away from each other. He rubbed at his neck, trying to appear casual while Cate tugged her hair in front of her face.

"Filled with food, water, lights, and other stuff, which might be helpful." He tossed a blue pack to Cate.

"I'm guessing limpy won't be able to carry anything. Jemma found this stick outside. The wood is smooth, and the end pointed so you can use it as a weapon and a cane. She says it came off of some kind of shovel, but who cares as long as it helps. What's with you two?"

"Nothing," Teddy said quickly and took the stick from his brother. He took a few tentative steps. "Not bad. Takes the weight off the foot. Not as good as those crutches we found, but they're somewhere in the tower."

"We going again?" Henri asked as he came back down the stairs. "Georges says I must go with you."

"Yeah, we have to find some medicine for Pa," Teddy said as Jolon handed the brute a pack. "Guess we better get going before Ma comes down and tries to talk us out of it."

After gathering some more supplies, they headed out. Jolon led the way and guided everyone back to the scrounger tunnel he, Nuna, and Cate used to enter Uppercity after Belinda took over the tower. By the time they found the room where they had stayed right after the invasion, Cate could see the trek had not been easy on Teddy. He sunk onto the ground and pulled out his water. After he had taken a long drink, he massaged his calf.

"Hey, you going to make it?" she asked as she sat beside him. For a moment, she wanted to caress his cheek, but she sat on her hands instead. The strange emotions and attraction were getting in the way. Ever since she re-joined the Peterson family, she couldn't get their kiss out of her mind.

"Yep," he grunted though his face was tight. "Just throbs a little."

"Where are we going?" Jolon asked, joining them.

Teddy pulled out the map from his back pocket, and Cate took it from him.

"Hey!"

"Oh, shush. Keep massaging that leg. I'll see what we're up to."

While she unfolded the map, she stuffed her emotions aside and banished the kiss from her thoughts.

Jolon shone his handlight on the paper, and she took a moment to figure out where they were.

"Looks like we have a fair way to go. The question is, do we go searching now or hunker down here until later?"

Something clattered in the hall, making them jump up. Jolon shone the light toward the door while Henri pulled out his gun.

"Whoever is there, come out. We're armed and ready for you," Jolon said, his voice shaking.

"Hey, it's me," said Cratchen as he stepped into the doorway with his hands in front of him.

Henri stuffed the gun away. "What you doing here?"

"Yeah, I thought Deb had your life all planned out," Cate said, pulling the kid in the room.

"Eh, she did, but she fell asleep reading, and I got bored, so I decided to help you guys."

Cate ruffled his hair. "I thought you said you didn't want to go back into the tunnels."

The kid took on a nonchalant pose, stuffing his hands in his pockets as he shrugged. "I get guilty knots when I should be doing something responsible. Don't know why. The skinny lady with the braids says it's my conscious or something like that. Can't say I believe her, but can't say I get what a conscious is either. Doesn't matter. Whatever it is, it nags me like an itch in my ear until I do something about it."

"You are one weird kid," Cate said with a laugh as she gave him a soft shove. "Glad to have you with us." She turned to the others. "He's a resourceful one."

"Yeah, okay, welcome to the club and all the wonderful words of joy you can think of. Some day we'll come up with an initiation ceremony for our pathetic little group, and you can earn a badge or something more interesting. For now, can we make a plan?" Jolon said with his usual exasperated frown. "I don't want to be here any longer than necessary."

"Right, well, anybody have an idea of when the market closes down?" Teddy asked, holding out his hand for the map.

Cate sat beside him and leaned over so they could both see. He made a face at her, and she returned the expression.

"Fine," he said with a hint of annoyance though she caught a flash of a quick grin.

"Market closes shortly after supper, which for most Upperlords is somewhere around six if you go by the clock in the square," the kid told them as he took a piece of cereal cake from Jolon.

"Anyone know what time it is?" Cate asked, and they all gave a negative response. "All right, so our first course of action is a snoop trip to check the time. This isn't going to be easy. Teddy's the only one who might pass as an Upperlord brat, but Dorkas and Belinda know what he looks like."

"Well, we're just going to have to risk it," Teddy said, getting to his feet. "Cratchen can go with me, and we'll be back as quick as we can." Right as he took his first step, he yelped and fell back.

"Yeah, this is good," Jolon said with a scowl. "You should have stayed back at the house."

"No, I'm fine. I just stepped wrong. I'll be more careful," he insisted, but Cate pushed him back.

"No point in stressing your foot if we don't have to. The kid and I can go. We'll slip in and slip out before anyone catches us."

"Come on, kid. You wanted adventure. This is it. Let's go," she said without waiting for Teddy's approval.

Chapter 11

Cate took a handlight but left her stash behind. As they stepped out in the hall, Henri caught up with her.

"What?" she asked, as he tugged on her arm.

The brute fidgeted about before pulling the gun out of his pocket. "Take this."

Surprised, she stared at the weapon. "Ah, no. I wouldn't be able to use it."

"I'll take it," the kid offered, holding out his hand, but Henri ignored him.

Henri put a hand on her shoulder his concern evident. "Be safe."

Uncomfortable with his show of affection, she patted his hand and stepped away. "Yeah. Okay. Don't worry, I'll be back."

"Both come back," he said with a nod and watched them go like a chicken losing its chicks.

"Okay, he's strange," the kid said as they made their way into the Upper hall.

"He cares, I guess."

As they joined the people milling about Uppercity, she pulled her hair over her eye. Uppers stared at her, and she tried to straighten her shirt, wishing she wore something better than cotton trousers and a plaid shirt.

"What's wrong?" Cratchen whispered.

"I don't blend in," she said as an elderly couple scanned her up and down, scorn plain on their faces.

"That's because you act like you don't. Glare back like they're the ones out of place."

Doubtful of his advice, she donned a haughty expression as they passed a whispering group of Uppers. Two of them met her gaze and rushed off while the others decided to be busy elsewhere. Pleased, Cate grinned, and Cratchen chuckled.

"Not bad. Uppers are all attitude. They think they are better, so they act like they're better, which makes other people think they are better. Treat them like they aren't and they get offended and run away."

"Or torture and kill you."

His lips spread in a wide grin. "Or that. So, we're heading to the clock, right? Might be best to go the back ways."

"The back ways?" she asked, pulling him aside to hide behind a pillar. "What back ways?"

"The servant halls. They weave about the different areas and take a little longer, but Uppers rarely ever go down them unless they don't want to be seen."

She paused and caught his sleeve. "What about brutes? I don't want to run into any of them either."

He glanced back behind them as three Uppers passed close by. "If we keep our heads down, we should be all right. Might work well if you fake a limp or a bent back."

"You're kidding, right?" she asked with a sceptical arch of her eyebrow.

"Doesn't hurt. The less appealing you make yourself, the further away people will want you."

"That makes sense. First, you say put on attitude, and then you say make yourself less appealing. Which do you want?"

"Be haughty when necessary and not when the time is right."

"Such helpful advice," she said and turned him around by his shoulders. "Which way?"

"Just follow and don't make eye contact," he advised as he led her to a rusted door. He pushed it open, and they entered a dim passage that stunk of urine. Underlings and brutes passed back and forth weary and sullen in their body language.

"How old are you again?" she asked as they went.

"Why?"

"Because you act so much older than you look."

The kid wrinkled his nose and bunched up his lips. "Don't most Underlings? I've been around Upper brats. They whine and complain about everything. Gets annoying. Can't stand them. Spent most of my life around adults. Even learned a little reading along the way. My second to last employer loved to sit and read aloud all day while I worked the stall. Made him so happy to condescendingly explained his babbling poetry as though I cared. Best part was he liked big words, and I got used to hearing them. Guess they just melted into my brain. Here, we turn here."

They left the hall behind and came out in the square where the lift to Undercity stood.

"Your people crippled the lift when they left," the kid said as they wove around the Underlings heading back to their horrible homes. "Was so funny. Took days to re-build it. Enjoyed that. Everyone was all so mad, running around cursing. All their pious stuck up masks fell away, and they squirmed. Really enjoyed that."

A soft chuckle escaped her lips as they reached the clock. The giant timepiece stood by the lift and reached up to the filthy ceiling windows.

"It's not running," she said, seeing the hands were stuck on four and two.

"Yeah, broke two nights ago," said an elderly brown woman with few wrinkles, but hints of grey hair. She clicked her tongue. "Some say 'twas the rebels. Others think them Uppers did it themselves to make us work longer."

Cate smacked a hand against her thigh. "Perfect. Well, we know it's still business hours," she said as they turned back. "If we wait a few hours, we could use the back ways to find this lab of Georges."

"She used to go through the back tunnels all the time," the kid said, leading her away. "Recognized her at your house. Hard to miss with such long braids. Don't forget one like her. Strange one. Tipsy one second serious the next. Was nice to me once. Gave me some food when my employer got mad at me and took my meal away."

"Sounds like Georges," Cate said while they moved back toward the passage to the others. "Guess she's not too well."

"Not surprising with all the drink. Most Uppers die from that junk. Don't like it much myself."

"You tried alcohol?" she asked with a sceptical glance his way.

"Yeah, a bunch of buds and me got a hold of a bottle and traded it about. Most of them loved it, but I hated the stuff. Hated the way it made me feel out of control. Gotta be in control. Never know who to trust."

"I get that," she said as they slipped through the door and into the back passage. "Been there myself."

The kid paused by the entrance and peered up at her, his eyes intense. "Thought so. You got that same thing about you. That's why I went along with you."

"So, what time is it?" Teddy asked as they came in.

Cate sat beside him and took another glance at the map. "The clock's dead. Apparently, someone decided they didn't like to follow it, but by the number of people wandering about, I'd say we have a couple of hours before the market closes."

"We'll never be able to tell here," he said, getting off the ground. "This place stinks of mould."

"Where do we go?" Henri asked, puzzled.

Jolon got up from his corner and held out his hand. "I know my opinion doesn't matter, but can I see the map?"

Teddy raised an eyebrow but handed the paper over.

Jolon shone his light on the sheet, turning the page until he uttered a satisfied, "Ah, ha."

"Yep, that's what I thought. Georges' lab is right in the heart of Belinda's tower. This won't be easy."

"You mean the place we went to with Nuna? The place where Dorkas went?" Cate asked.

"Right building different floor. It's hard to say. Maybe we could hide out there."

Cate nodded as a chunk of slime slid down one of the walls and stirred up a disgusting stench. "At least, it's not this stinking hole."

"It's amazing, isn't it?" Teddy said with a laugh.

"What?" she asked with a frown, wondering if he was laughing at her.

He flicked his hand up. "How fast we got used to air, space, and a healthy place to be."

She leaned toward him. "Are you saying we're getting soft?"

With a quick smile, he caught her hand. "Yep. I don't mind, do you?"

Pressing her lips together, she pondered whether or not he meant the hand holding or getting soft. "Yeah," she answered, not caring which way he took it. Before she could decide otherwise, she stepped forward and kissed his lips. "Let's go."

She pulled her hand out of his and left the room with the kid following behind, a sly expression on his face. Henri went after them his face blank as though he was thinking of someone else.

Jolon slapped Teddy on the back. "What a fascinating turn of events. Something you want to share?"

"Nope," he said, taking his brother's hand and getting off the floor. "Every time I think I have her figured out, she sneaks in and surprises me. Was nice, though."

"Eh, don't," Jolon said, his lip curled in displeasure.

"You've never been a romantic soul, have you?" Teddy asked as they trailed after the others.

His brother stuffed his hands in his pockets and sauntered along as though on a careless stroll. "Not my thing. I don't mind people, but physical attraction never drew me in. I like being with people, girls, hold hands, chat, that sort of stuff. That's enough."

"If you say so."

"Bothers you?"

Teddy shrugged. "No. Everyone has different preferences. Not my business. I have enough trouble sorting out my own life." As they fell behind, he tried to move faster and catch up with the others. His ankle didn't hurt, but he wasn't ready to go skipping yet.

"Where are we going?"

"Told you, the passages that Dorkas went through," he replied with a wry grin as though Teddy should know where that was.

"Yeah, thanks. Guess I'll have to trust you," Teddy said, looping his arm over his brother's shoulder. "Hey, I know we give you a hard time, but I do try to listen to you."

"Right," his brother said as though he didn't believe him.

"I do," Teddy insisted with a squeeze to Jolon's shoulder as they slipped through the square. "And I promise to be nicer in the future if we survive this."

Jolon gave a sharp laugh. "Ooh, there's something to look forward to. I thought you were dead, you know."

"What?" Teddy asked, taken back by the confession.

His brother cleared his throat, his gaze on the floor. "Yeah, when we were all separated. I thought you were all gone like everyone else in my past. Didn't feel too good."

"No," Teddy said with a sideways hug. "I was worried about you too. Didn't...don't want to lose you."

"Mmm," Jolon grunted as though he didn't trust himself to speak. "We're, ah, umm, we're almost there. I ought to catch up and lead the way."

Teddy grinned at his brother. "Let's go."

After they had reached the others, Jolon led them down a back hallway with few people in it. He stopped at a spot where the passage split off in two directions. An old poster of a large head with a blue tongue and a bottle of blue liquid was framed in faded gold metal and protected behind glass. The words 'now playing' were posted in large letters across the bottom.

"Let's see that map again," Jolon asked, and Teddy handed it over. "For an Upperlord, Georges has terrible writing and drawing skills. This stuff's all squiggly." He tilted the paper toward the others. "This is a tunnel, yes?"

Teddy peered at the drawing. "I think so. Yes."

"That's what I thought. See, that's the ugly poster, right? Now playing, that's what she has written here, right? I remembered it from the last time I was here. You can't see something that ugly and forget it. Keeps coming back to me in the night. The last time, it turned all my food blue and ate it. Couldn't stop it. Gave me cold sweats."

Cate flicked him lightly on the back of the head. "You are so weird."

"Hey," he protested, rubbing his head.

"In a good way; in a good way," she said with her hands raised.

"So, we go that way?" Henri asked, pointed down the tunnel.

"Looks like it." He turned and went down the hall, following the map. "We should come up to another small square."

Cate pulled him back by his shirt. "Voices," she said in low tones, and they all stopped. "We should probably find a place to wait until these Uppers clear out."

Caden paced the den, restlessly flipping through magazine pages and tossing about books.

"I was wondering where you went," Nuna said as she came in. "Your mother wanted assurances that you were all right. I told her I would check on you."

"How's Pa?" she asked, not wanting to discuss herself.

"Better," she said as she sat in a dark brown armchair. She wove her fingers together and held her hands in front of her, elbows propped on the chair.

"Jemma and your mother have been washing his wound frequently and changing his bandages. His fever is down too, which is a good sign."

The muscles in Caden's throat tightened. Lightheaded, she collapsed on a padded bench under the window and swallowed to keep herself from crying.

"That's good. That's good. I'm glad."

A trinket of a porcelain cat lay on the counter, and she picked it up, twisting it around and around in her hands until she dropped it, chipping of an ear. Her tongue felt swollen. As her anxiety rose, she clenched her jaw and pressed her fingers firmly together.

Nuna moved beside her and put an arm around her shoulders. For a long while, neither of them said anything. She had no strength left to push the affection away.

"I'm tired," Caden whispered, resting her head against the woman's shoulder.

"I know," Nuna said, stroking her hair.

"It's a knotted mess."

"Yes, a horrible, evil mess that seems impossible to fix."

Snuffling, Caden lifted her head and met the woman's gaze. She tugged at a lock. "I meant my hair," she said, and a reckless bubble of laughter rose up inside her. She hiccupped and giggled, feeling off center.

Nuna grinned and hugged her tight. "Well, that's a problem we can fix." She examined a matted clump. "Though I think we might have to do a drastic cut."

A long sigh coursed through Caden's chest as the tension in her released a little. "Don't mind that. Might feel good."

"Come on," the woman said as she got up with a firm grip on Caden's hand. "There are scissors in the kitchen."

Jemma was there when they entered, her hair tied up in a soft grey scarf with pale pink flowers. Evening sunlight streamed in through the open window over the sink and a gentle wind brought in the scent of the outdoors.

"Hello," Jemma greeted as she stirred a cup of something. "Would you like some tea? I found some honey. Though it's turned to crystal, so it takes a bit of stirring."

"A cup for both of us, dear," Nuna said as she sat Caden down on a stool and fished a pair of scissors out of a drawer. "There we are. These will do."

"Ah, time for a trim, is it?" Jemma asked as she prepared the drinks.

Caden scrubbed away the tear that snuck from her eye. "Let's go for something new. Cut it all away and start over," she said as brightly as she could muster.

"Ah, yes, good idea. I've done that a few times over the years." Jemma said with a supportive nod. "Nuna's good with the scissors. She'll trim you up just right."

She handed each of them a cup, and Nuna put hers on the kitchen table after she had a sip. "Good. Refreshing. Thanks."

Jemma pulled over another stool and perched by the counter. "Go on, try some," she encouraged, and Caden took a sip.

The sweet drink soothed her throat and unwound the knots in her chest. She put the cup aside as Nuna started to cut away her hair.

"Change is good. Helps you see things from different angles," Jemma said. She opened a tin and offered her a cookie. "Want one? Tastes good dipped in the tea."

"Thanks, maybe after," she said as her hair fell in piles around her.

"Oh, this is going well," Nuna declared, pausing to view her work.

As she hopped off her stool, Jemma dusted crumbs off her pants. "I'll get a mirror. There's one on Georges' dresser upstairs. I think you'll like the results."

"I'm glad you two are back together," Caden said as Nuna brushed the hair from her shoulders with a towel.

"Me too," she answered with a quiet snicker. "Though I think I'm still harboring a hint of anger deep in my bones. She got lost. I'm not surprised. She gets thinking of things and doesn't pay attention to where she's going."

"Pa's like that," Caden choked as her voice caught.

The woman patted her leg. "He's going to be fine, dear. The others will find the medicine and bring it back."

"Yeah," she said and sighed.

"Hey, Teddy," Cate called as they sat in a service closet waiting for their chance to move.

"Huh?" he said, waking from the stupor of sleep. He scrunched his face in an effort to wake up, and she tried not to find it adorable.

"It's been quiet for a while. And I think by the weariness in my bones it's gotten late. We should get moving."

"Right," he said as he got off the floor and helped her up too.

The four of them slipped out of the closet and into the dim hall.

"Which way?" Henri asked, stretching his bulky muscles.

"Somewhere to pee," Jolon muttered, shifting about.

"Use the bucket in the closet," Cate told him and he went back in the little room, closing the door behind him.

"I go too," Henri said after Jolon came out.

Cate rolled her eyes. "Well, we might as well all go. Wouldn't want to wet ourselves while robbing the lab."

Teddy laughed and took his turn. She waited until he was back and went in, holding her breath as the room stunk. After she had relieved herself, she covered the pail with a plastic bag and brought it with her.

"Seriously?" Jolon asked at the sight of the bucket and a mop. "Why are you bringing that?"

"We need a distraction, remember? There is nothing more distracting than a bucket of piss." She handed him the mop and passed the pail to Henri.

The brute grimaced and took it, holding the bucket of urine as far away from his body as he could.

After taking out the map, Teddy led them through the square and down another hall to an elevator.

"Now what?" Jolon asked as they stopped.

He studied the map. "We go down."

"What?" Cate asked, peering over his shoulder at the map. "How? Elevators don't work."

"The map says we take the elevator. That's all I know."

"How do we open it?" she asked as she studied the solid, closed doors with no visible handles.

Teddy pressed a small round button on the wall, and it lit up. He shrugged a shoulder in an almost apologetic way. "It has a down arrow on it."

"Always practical, eh, clever boy?" she said with a grudging grin.

"Clever boy; I like that better than old guy," he replied, his golden eyes bright.

"Oh, pick a better time to flirt," Jolon said, stepping between them. "Either this thing is coming, or the building is about to fall apart," he added as a rumbling came from behind the doors.

Everyone braced themselves, glancing at each other as though they expected the floor to collapse. A tiny bell dinged, and the doors chugged open.

"In we go?" Jolon said, stepping over the metal threshold.

They followed him in and stood there in the tiny room as the doors shut.

"Press a button," Cate said as she nudged Teddy.

"Right. Which one?" he asked, rubbing his fingertips together.

"One that takes us down?" Jolon suggested.

"Or one that gets us out of here," the kid offered, half hiding behind Henri's leg.

Teddy grimaced and pushed a button marked with a B. "B for back or b for basement. Basement makes more sense. Right"

The box lurched downward, and Cate's stomach went in the other direction. Instinctively, she grasped Teddy's hand while he clutched hers in turn.

They watched in silence as the machine began to move and the numbers above the door lit up one after the other. When the elevator jerked to an unexpected stop, everyone yelped and huddled together.

"Fun," Henri said though his eyes blinked rapidly.

Cate stepped into the darkness, her eye adjusting to the low light. "Now what?"

Behind them, the elevator doors closed. Cate twisted around, surprised by the automated action from the inanimate object. The lights above the door flickered and moved as the numbers went up.

"It moving," Henri said, his mouth open as he gaped at the doors.

"No, really, big guy?" Jolon said, backing away from the lift, his brow creased with worry. "Here I thought it was us."

"Do you think someone else is coming?" Cate asked as the numbers stopped changing for a moment then began to go back down.

"Yep," Jolon said and held the mop out in front of him like a weapon. He shrugged when the others stared at him.

"Gotta do something."

"Let's hide," Teddy suggested and pulled Cate around the darker side of the elevator. The others joined them, and they huddled together just as the bell dinged, and the doors opened.

Two Underlings came out pushing a cart filled with food. Before anyone made any move, Henri stepped out and grabbed them. He bonked their heads together and dumped them, dazed, in a corner.

A short, hairy one blinked and yelped, but Jolon whacked him on the head with his stick, and he slumped down. Meanwhile, Henri punched the second one in the face, and his head went back, striking the brick wall. The Underling fell on top of the other guy, and they both lay still.

Stunned, Cate and Teddy stared at them.

"Part of plan, right?" Henri said with a sheepish shrug.

Jolon stood there, wide-eyed and gaping. "I didn't kill him, did I? Never hit anyone before. It's, well," his throat apple bobbed up and down as he swallowed. "I think I could do it again," he said though he didn't look too confident.

"Good, cause you might have to," Teddy said with a chuckle and placed the bucket on the bottom shelf of the cart. "You two find a place to hide them while Cate and I take the cart and try to find this lab. Cratchen, you stay here and watch the elevator."

"You move 'em. I'll search for a cubbyhole to stuff them in," Jolon said as Henri grabbed each Underling by a foot and dragged them across the ground.

The kid snickered and made himself invisible in the shadows.

"So, what is your plan?" Teddy asked as Cate took the mop and went with him.

"Simple. You bring in the cart. I'll follow behind and dump the bucket someplace away from the meds. While I overdo the clean-up, you grab what you can and then we'll bolt."

"Right, does sound simple. It will either work or get us thrown in the pits," he said as they drew close to the lab.

The sight of the two lumbering brutes on either side of the door made them falter in their steps, but they clasped fingers for a moment and kept going. The round-faced brute to the left walked in front of them with his meaty hand up.

"Where are Jake and Tyron?" he asked, squinting at them with deep brown eyes.

"Uh, don't know," Teddy said with a disinterested shrug. "Just got orders to bring the cart down."

The chalky grey brute on the right pawed at his beard and stepped toward Cate. She knew the lust in his eyes and cringed, anger welling inside.

"And you? You here to deliver food?" the creeper brute asked in a way that made her skin want to leave. He scanned her up and down, his blood-red lips parted in a disgusting sneer.

Behind her in the shadows, she could sense the presence of others. Her breath quickened as she hoped it was Henri and Jolon.

"Keme?" Henri said as he stepped out of the dark.

The square face of the brute to the right brightened with friendly recognition, his grey-gold eyes smiling. "Henri? Well, where have you been? I thought you disappeared with Upperlord Georges."

"I did," Henri replied with an open grin. "But she assigned me to the Petersons. These two are in my protection."

"Your protection?" the left brute squealed, his lips twisted in disgust. "They ain't nothing, but a couple of Under brats. Brutes don't protect their kind." He snickered, drawing himself up. "You are a traitor to the Upperlords and the brute society. I won't be surprised if they roast you slowly and let the rats eat you. You snivelling, pathetic...."

Keme's fist slammed into the side of his head, knocking him sense-less. "He talks too much. Don't like him much." A grin spread across his ruddy-brown face as he smoothed back his dark brown hair. "So what are you up to?"

"I thought you dead," Henri said, laughing. They hugged like broth-ers, slapping each other on the back.

The guard grasped Henri's biceps, holding him at a distance. "Ah, I thought you were too. I kept searching for you, hoping you wouldn't end up a brute or worse. But Upperlord Belinda sold me to the medic, and he assigned me here. There are about a dozen of us who live down here and guard on a two-hour rotation. Rarely see anyone except their ugly mugs. Been defending this place with that toad for years. Happy to see a friendly face."

"We need medicine," Teddy cut in as the brute on the floor groaned.

Henri's friend kicked the toad in the head, and he went still again. "Don't worry. He'll be fine. End up hitting him at least once a night. Got a head hard as stone and twice as thick. So, you need medicine, and you've come here to get it. Brave."

"Don't have much choice," Jolon said, joining Teddy. He trembled as though wary. "Pa's dying. He needs our help."

"True. He good person too," Henri told him. He put his arms around Teddy and Jolon. "They family. You family. You help."

The man licked his lips and nodded. "I missed you, friend. Get your medicine. I'll keep the way clear. There are three lab rats in there, but they're a cowardly bunch. Though they will put up a stink if you rile them. The others will come running if they call out for help. My re-placement will be here soon as it is."

"Come on, Teddy. Henri and Jolon can wait out here," Cate said as he hesitated as though he had doubts. "If there is any trouble, they'll let us know."

"We don't have much choice," Jolon added though he looked as though he would rather eat rats.

Teddy nodded and slung his stash on his back. "Fine. Let's do this."

Henri grabbed Cate's arm and held out his gun. "Take this."

She stared at the weapon, her fingers twitching. "Yeah, okay. So you just pull the trigger, right?"

He nodded and placed it in her hand. "Sort of. But, it empty. Checked earlier. No more bullets. Safety still on, in case, but empty."

Chuckling, she took the gun and put it in her jacket pocket. "I guess I could always throw it at someone."

Keme stepped aside and pushed the door open while Jolon and Henri crept into the shadows.

Cate and Teddy entered the lab, which was a bright room with many lights hanging down in strips from the ceiling. Several cabinets with glass doors ran down all the walls. Inside each, were bottles and jars of all sorts of sizes. At the far end, were the three lab rats that Keme mentioned, each bent over their desks, scribbling in books and staring into strange instruments.

"How are we going to find the medicine we need amid all of this?" she whispered as they pushed the cart further into the room.

"Just get the bucket," Teddy hissed back.

She pulled the pail of pee out from under the cart and followed behind as he went around a wide counter and approached the first lab person.

"Food's here," he said, and the lab medic sat up, turning her narrow head to face him.

"Who are you?" she demanded, rising from her stool. Her wiry dark brows drew together and made her harsh face seem longer.

Her colleague stomped over, all business and bluster. "I know you," he said, crossing his arms over his thick stomach and staring at Teddy.

"I, ahh," He stumbled over his words and put his hands up in denial. "Don't think so."

"He's one of the rebels," said the mousy third person with narrow eyes and wide cheeks. "Saw him when Belinda caught them. His pa's the one I got stored in the clinic."

Teddy faltered, a flush of heat rushing up his neck as his expression turned angry. " Mm... my...."

"He ain't got no father," Cate interjected, hoping to give Teddy time to recover. She moved away from them, slipping around the other side of the counter. Casually, she put the bucket on top. "Ah, I don't know what you lab types are talking about. Bren has been shifting about with me for two years now."

"Don't listen to her," the mousy guy said, jabbing a finger at her. "I know that's where he's from."

"What are you doing here," the woman demanded, her eyes wide and cross.

"Bren," Cate shrieked, turning toward him. "You rat. You've been cheating on me? How dare you?"

She stepped forward and smacked him on the arm. He stared at her, protesting his innocence.

"You liar. I knew something was up. You said you were just hanging with old Grider. All this time...."

She wound up and swung her arm wide, hitting the bucket. The foul water sprayed all over the lab food and all over harsh face and thick belly. They shouted and moved away.

"Oh, I'm sorry," she gasped while Teddy caught on and moved back toward the cabinets. She grabbed some napkins from the cart, smacking into the pitcher and a plate, sending both flying.

"Ah, you clumsy piece of garbage," shouted mousy. He backed away as she whipped around her mop.

"Don't worry, I'll get it," she insisted, blocking thick belly's way with the cart as he tried to pass. She wanted to give Teddy as much time as possible.

"What are you doing over there?" harsh face asked, then gasped and ducked as Cate whirled around with the mop.

"Please, let me just clean it up," she insisted, pushing the cart into mousy.

A plate of noodles slid off and splatted on his shirt. "Oh, no," she exclaimed and tossed the mop aside. She tore another napkin from the cart and tried to dabble him, but he backed up, slipped on the pee-soaked floor and went down, taking harsh face with him.

"I'll just go and get you more food," Cate said, backing up with the cart. "Bren, let's go and get them a fresh cart. We'll have to bring back a fresh pail of water too."

"Stop," shouted thick belly. "Stop, guards!"

"Quiet," Cate yelled, pulling out the gun. They stepped back; harsh face ducked behind the counter, and thick belly hid behind a tray.

She whirled around and ran, pulling on Teddy's arm as she went. "I hope you got what you needed, cause we're done."

They bolted through the door and nearly ran into the others.

"Come on," they both said and tore off toward the elevator.

"This way," Keme exclaimed as he rushed past them. "If you try to take the elevator, they'll catch you."

"Hey," the kid yelled as they went past. "Don't leave me behind."

"Get moving, then." Cate ordered, and Henri grabbed the kid by the shirt and hauled him off.

Behind them, they could hear shouts and the sound of several booted feet coming after them. Cate didn't waste time or energy checking on who was following; she kept her eye on Keme and kept going.

Chapter 12

Everyone rushed down hall after hall, slipping through so many doors Cate lost track of where they were. She stumbled and gasped as she collided with a box hidden from her view.

Jolon collapsed beside her, panting and holding his side. "Did we lose them?"

Henri grasped Keme's arm while the kid slid off his back. "All good?"

"Should be," the other brute said. "These tunnels weave all over, and I tried to go through many different doors so that no one can track us. Though I don't know how I'll explain this to anyone. Guess my guard days are over."

"Sorry, Keme," Teddy said, patting the man on the arm. "Didn't mean to get you in trouble."

"Hey, I did it by choice," he said with a broad grin.

"Why did you?"

He blinked at Cate. "What?"

"I understand you are friends with Henri, but why help us? As far as you know this is it, right?"

"What do you mean?" he asked, staring down at her. Whether to intimidate her or out of true confusion, she wasn't sure.

"We told him," Jolon cut in.

"Told him what?" Teddy asked.

"About outside," Henri answered and put a hand on his friend's shoulder. "We care for each other so long. He friend I thought lost. He like outside. I know."

"I watched over Henri for a long time, growing up. He's my little brother, and I've got him back. Where he goes, I go."

"This is wonderful," Jolon said, getting off the floor. "All cheerful and mushy, and so not helpful right now. The reunion is touching. Can we get out of this hole and get the medicine back to Pa?" He turned to Teddy. "You got the medicine, yes?"

"Yeah, pretty much. Grabbed what I could plus a few extras. Could only find one bag of blood, though. Hope it's enough."

"Come on," Keme said and guided them forward with Henri by his side.

Cate kept her attention on them, still wary of his participation.

"Don't trust him," the kid said, falling into step beside her. "Just met him. He's a brute. They're mean. Uh, not Henri, but the others are all mean. A brute's life is sweet compared other Underlings. Get their own places, special food, and anything Upperlords don't want. Sure, Uppers sell and trade 'em, but that ain't much compared to the privileges they get."

"Yeah well, it seems I have a habit of attracting instant heroes."

"What's that?"

"An instant hero? Someone like you who seems to do all the right things right when I need it."

"Maybe it's fate," Teddy said, walking on her blind side.

She slowed a step and turned untill he came into her view. Somewhere during their flight, he had lost his cane and now favoured his damaged ankle.

For a moment, she wanted to offer him some help—her arm around his shoulder and his arm around his waist—the thoughts that followed this image caused too many inconvenient emotions. Instead, she folded her arms over her chest and let him get along on his own.

"What's fate?" the kid asked.

"Fate is this idea or energy that puts things into place so that life will either get better or get worse. Each person, each situation arises like different passages in the tunnels. Which way things go depends on which path you choose. Sometimes it works out and sometimes it doesn't. Cate, you could have ignored Cratchen when you stumbled over him. Doesn't mean you wouldn't have found Pa, but it doesn't mean you would have, either. Also, he could have ignored you or turned you in to some Upperlord or brute."

"So, each event could have gone differently depending on the choices we all made individually," she said.

"Seems silly. Things just are. Everything's all luck," the kid said, making a face. "Getting out of here is up to us, our smarts, and lots of luck."

"Yeah, and we're not out of here yet, so that stuff all doesn't matter," Cate said, searching for some sign of an escape route as they caught up with Henri. " We need an exit."

Keme scratched his head. "There's a passage to Upper..."

"No. We need an exit to outside," she said, and he stopped in the middle of the hall.

His face froze, mouth open and eyes wide. "Ahh... no. That's, that's...."

"Possible. Completely possible." Cate confronted him, standing in front of his thick barrel chest. "We've gone outside." She swept a hand toward the others. "All of us, and we lived. No, we didn't just live we got better. So, don't balk, don't stutter and run. Lead us out of this pit and find an exit."

"Uh... ah." The brute ran his hands through his hair then slapped his thigh. "Okay. Ummm. There's a, an exit down that way." He gestured toward a passage to their right. "It's sealed, but I can probably get it open with Henri's help."

"And it goes outside?" Jolon asked.

Keme shifted from foot to foot as though he wanted to run in the other direction. "Yes, at least, that is what everyone has always believed. No one has ever opened it to check for certain."

Despite his fears, he led everyone down the passage through areas that grew darker and colder as they went.

"The exit is this way," Keme pointed toward a wide staircase to the left. "No one's ever gone up here in a long time, but it's the closest exit I can think of." Every ounce of colour left his features.

At the top of the stairs, they came to a set of metal doors secured by several steel beams wedged between the floor and the doors. Keme and Henri removed the girders quietly so as not to alert anyone of their whereabouts. After, they pushed the doors open, and moonlight flooded the passage.

Keme hugged the wall, his eyes screwed shut and his chest unmoving. Henri clapped a hand on his shoulder.

"It's good. See?" As he stepped out, a light breeze played with his hair and the light brightened his skin.

The other brute gasped and followed, his limbs shaking like he was ready to fall apart. After a few moments and several hesitant steps, a grin crept onto Keme's lips, spreading them wide across his face.

"Not so bad, is it?" Cate asked as she passed him. "Now, we just gotta find home."

By the time they reached the house, the sun had peeked over the horizon. Despite his ankle, Teddy rushed in with the medical supplies and headed up the stairs.

"Ma, Ma? I've got it. We got the stuff."

"Oh, good, thank you," Ma said as she ran into the hall and snatched the bag from him. A heavy exhale slipped through her lips—worry and fear etched into her features. She rummaged through the supplies, her brow furrowing deeper. "Georges, help me. I don't know what to do with all this."

The Upperlord came from her room, and they went in to see Pa, closing the door behind them.

Teddy waited outside for a moment, hesitating. He wanted to see his father but was terrified to find him broken, dying.

"Good to have you back," Caden said, showing up beside him. "Everything went well?"

"Not bad. Picked up another follower," he said absently, his fingertips pressed against the door.

"Come on." With a tug to his shirt, she pulled him into her room and shoved him onto the bed. "Don't linger. Doesn't help." She rubbed her arms and dropped beside him. "Noticed the new addition. Another brute, interesting."

"Yeah, a friend of Henri's." He rested against the head of the bed and propped his leg up. "Seems they grew up together before the whole brute thing."

"Ah, yeah, Kim or Cam or something like that."

"Keme."

"Right. Henri mentioned him a couple of times. How's the leg?"

"Aches. Had to run, and that didn't go well. How's Pa?"

She lay across the bed and hugged a pillow. "Don't know. Ma hasn't left his room, and they won't let anyone else in."

"Anyone hungry?" Jolon asked as he came in with Cate behind him. He put a tray filled with food on the bedside table and passed each of them a bowl. "It's more of Jemma's cereal."

"Thanks," Teddy said as he took his food. A loud grumble came from his stomach, reminding him he hadn't eaten for quite a while.

"Where are the others?" he asked as he scooped up a spoonful of food.

"Henri and Keme are catching up, and the kid is sleeping, I think. Jemma's making food, and Nuna's helping Ma," Jolon said as he hopped onto the dresser and dug into his food.

"So, what do we do now?" Teddy asked while Cate moved over to the other side of the room and sat in a chair by the window. Sunlight filtered in, making long shadows.

"Sleep," Jolon said between mouthfuls. "My eyes are drilling holes into my head I'm so tired."

"Go back," Cate said, putting her bowl aside.

Caden sat up, her attention all on the other girl.

"Why would we want to do that?" Jolon asked, his mouth twisting as though he tasted something terrible.

A dark scowl crossed her brow. "You know why."

"Yeah, probably," he said, jerking a shoulder up. "But I'm surprised you do."

"If we go back, we go back with just us," Caden said, standing. "Henri and his friend stay to protect the others." She pointed toward Teddy. "Those Uppers recognized you. Belinda will come after us. Maybe not today, but the creepers and brutes will come once they realize they can go outside. And if we go back, we do whatever we can to let everyone know they are free to go outside and live."

"Well, you don't want much," Teddy said, and he had to grin at the idea. "What I want is to find Dorkas and get some answers, but we'll need Henri and Keme to do this."

She shook her head. "They should stay. If this all goes bad and the Uppers come looking for us, they will need someone here to protect them."

"All right, people," Jolon exclaimed as he hopped off the dresser. "How about we get a couple of hours of sleep and plan from there? Uppercity isn't going anywhere"

"And the rest of the tower people are probably already dead. That's what you're thinking, isn't it?" Teddy said and the words sank like a brick in his stomach.

"And I'm so tired I can't think straight," Jolon said as he ran his hands over his face. He wandered out of the room. "Wake me when you're ready."

"Yeah, me too," Cate said with a yawn, and she left, giving Teddy a light smile on the way out.

"That's interesting," Caden said with a soft snicker. "You two...."

"We two what?" Teddy asked, shifting uncomfortably.

A smirk spread across her face. "Nothing. You really think they're all dead?"

"Don't know," he said as his chest tightened. He folded his arms and rubbed his arms over his biceps.

"Sleep. That was a long night last night, and tonight will probably be even longer," Caden said and ruffled his hair. "I don't think they're dead. Don't know why, but I think they're still alive and I'm going back to find them. Now, I'm going to fill the packs and collect some stuff for the trip back. But first, I want to have a talk with our new friend."

"Be kind," he said as he wrapped himself in a blanket and drifted off, letting sleep give him a moment's reprieve.

Caden went downstairs and out to the backyard where Henri and Keme sat on the porch, talking.

"Hey, Henri, why don't you get Keme some food?"

He glanced up at her, his cheeks flushing. "Already did. You good? Like hair."

Pleased he noticed, she put a hand to her shorn locks. "Thanks. Easier to deal with. Get some sleep, please? I'd like to chat with your friend. Get to know him."

Confused, he brought his eyebrows together. "Oh, uh, okay."

After he had left, she sat across from Keme and studied him. He was a typical brute in build, but more like Nuna with straight black hair and ruddy skin. His forehead was broad, and his brow loomed heavy over deep brown eyes. The man seemed nervous as he played with a leaf, twirling it about between his fingers, his gaze troubled and his lips twitching. Despite her suspicious nature, she put it down to the shock of being outside.

"So, you're the Keme Henri said was his best friend growing up," she said, hoping to put him at ease.

"And you must be Caden. The one Henri is quite taken with."

"Quite taken with?" she repeated with a tilt of her head. "As in he likes me? I guess. You speak well for a brute. You and Teddy would have fun in a word war."

"I like books. My first keeper was an Upper with an old grandfather who liked to be read to. He took my broken speech as a personal affront, and I was young and didn't mind. Henri has improved. The most he used to say was 'k.'"

A couple of pink petals drifted down from a nearby tree, and she brushed them from her lap. "Teddy's been teaching him."

The brute nodded, rubbing his palms together. "Good. He's smart in his own way."

She leaned against the banister and wrapped her arms around her knees. "Yeah, he's never made a good brute. Heart's too big."

"I know. I lost track of him after they took me away. Uppers don't like the brutes to mingle too much, especially the smart ones—might start making plans. Never wanted Henri to become a brute. But then, I never planned on staying a brute myself. I was just waiting for the right opportunity to change."

Suspicions tweaked in her gut; she propped her head against her hand. "Opportunity? What opportunities are there in Uppercity for brutes? A better keeper? Guarding the greenhouses?"

"I don't know," he said, his gaze far away and troubled. "This may be it?"

"This?" she asked, glancing about the yard.

"I would say so." He waved a hand out over the beauty of the back-yard. "This is worth change; wouldn't you say?"

"It is to me," she said, wanting to take him at his words, but something still didn't seem right.

"I spent most of the last few years in the bowels of Uppercity. The air down there is dry; gives me nosebleeds. The brutes I had to work with are, well, the worst sort of mould. I have no problem leaving them behind."

"Ah, huh. That's good. So, where are they hiding the others from the tower?" She threw the question in quickly, watching close for his reaction.

Keme stood and stepped out on the ground. "I have heard of them, yes, but I'm not certain where they are." As he bent down, he ran his hands over the grass before plucking a tiny purple flower.

Was he avoiding her gaze or just fascinated by the foliage. She couldn't tell.

"But they are still alive."

"Yes. Though after the raid on the pharmacy, I can't say for how much longer."

"Well, it would be wonderful to destroy Undercity, set everyone free, and save the world. That sort of thing. For now, we need to find our people and let as many of them as we can know it's safe to go outside along the way."

"Ah, you don't want much, do you?" he said with an odd laugh. "But I get it."

"Do you? I'm not a trusting person like Henri. You helped us out, and I appreciate that, but..."

The brute tossed his flower aside and hooked his fingers in the waistband of his pants. "I left everything behind. The Upperlords know

I helped and don't appreciate disloyalty." His chest heaved as he inhaled and met her gaze for a flick of a second. "You don't trust me, and I am not surprised. If it weren't for Henri, I would have probably turned you in, but now..." he spread his arms wide, palms up. "This is hope."

"Can't argue with that," she said though she though his words sounded hollow.

"Are they dead?" she asked, watching him closely. "The rest of the people from the tower, do you think they are already dead?"

He sighed, his shoulders sagging. "It's possible, but nobody moves too fast in Uppercity. If they are alive, your group is probably hiding in the dungeon."

"The dungeon? Where the pharmacy is?"

Keme joined her on the step. "No. Close, but no. There's a passage, which leads to this... I guess it's a room if you push the definition. When Uppers want to make a public display, they use the pits. When they want to hide someone, they throw them in there. It's a place of putrid water dripping down the walls and bug-infested garbage and... nothing good." His words came out slow as though he had no choice but to share them.

As she stood, she dusted herself off. "Fine, then that's where we'll go. Works for me."

"But it's too dangerous. You don't know the way," he said, running a hand through his short hair.

"Draw us a map. The others need protection. You and Henri need to stay here."

"Not a good idea," he protested, moving toward her.

"There aren't any good ideas anymore; didn't you know? If this doesn't work, this family will be alone. There will be no one to protect the kids or help our parents. They need you and Henri."

"But if we go with you, the plan has a better chance of working."

Caden waved a finger at him. "Clever, but still not a good idea."

"Think about it," he said, staring down at her in such a condescending manner, she wanted to poke him.

Irritated, she tapped her fingers against her leg, wishing he would listen. "I'll do that. Coming in? Henri's probably wondering where we are."

"Ah, I'll stay out here for a while." He stepped out onto the grass again and gazed at the sky.

Caden headed back inside and busied herself with cleaning up. After, Deb wanted to go for a walk, so they went with Jemma to get more water. The late afternoon was warm and fragrant with little birds and tiny creatures with bushy tails that Deb said were squirrels according to her books.

Books, everyone seemed to have books filled with the most amazing information. What difference did it make if one called the animals squirrels or brown fuzzies?

When they got back, Ma was downstairs sitting on the couch while Georges rested beside her.

"Tisha, you have to relax now," Georges was saying while Ma fussed. "Nuna is with Tru, and he is responding well to treatment. You won't do anyone any good if you exhaust yourself."

"She's right, Ma," Caden said as she rested a hand on her mother's shoulder. "You've been up since yesterday. You must be exhausted. I'll go up and check on him. The others are back. We have food and a good home. Rest."

Ma nodded and collapsed in on herself. "Fine. I just... I...."

"Sleep," Caden insisted, giving her mother a kiss on the forehead.

Her mother lay back and closed her eyes. Caden pulled a blanket over her and left her there with Georges. She went upstairs and hesitated before entering her father's room. Curtains covered the windows, allowing only dim slits of evening light through. Nuna sat in a chair beside his bed. Pa lay there with strange tubes attached to his arms, his face so pale he almost seemed see-through.

"How is he?" she asked quietly, moving to the other side of the bed.

"No telling," Nuna whispered. "The infection is clearing, and his fluids are better. Took a bit to figure out how to attach the bags, but we got everything set up with Georges' help. He's been asleep for a while now, which is good. Rest is the best medicine now."

"I want to stay with him for a while," she said, and Nuna got up from her chair.

"Of course, I'll leave you two. I could use to relieve myself and get some food. Might close my eyes for a moment or two."

Caden took Nuna's chair as the woman left. Limbs shaking and eyes stinging, she took her father's hand, his once strong fingers slack and fragile in hers.

A couple of hours later, Cate sat on the back porch with Teddy, Caden, and Jolon while Keme offered up all the knowledge he possessed about the passages of Undercity. Cratchen was awake and splayed out on the grass, plucking tiny yellow flowers.

"I ain't going back," Cratchen said as though he expected them to ask him.

"We know, kid," Cate said and tossed a tiny twig at him. "We aren't asking you to."

He fidgeted and got to his feet, hands stuck in his pockets. "I ain't."

"Yes, Crat. Go find Deb. We got this," Jolon said, waving the kid away.

Cratchen shuffled about before stomping away.

Henri came out and sat between Cate and Caden, his face all warped by concern. "Don't go without me."

"You have to stay," Caden said, grasping his forearm.

"No," he said, his frustration raising his voice in pitch.

"Henri...." Caden started, but he cut her off.

"No." He stood, pacing. "Not good idea. Don't like it. I go, or no one goes."

"You can't stop us," Caden insisted, standing in front of him. "I'm not yours to protect. Even if we were together in any way other than friends, I still wouldn't be yours to order about."

The brute stared at her, his hands flexing open and close. "You no fair."

She couldn't hold back her exasperated laugh. "Nothing is fair. That's the problem. We're split nine ways to hell with few options that sound even close to good. Do we leave them there? Is that what you want? Sure we can all set up house here, but we will always wonder if they will find us. Besides, I don't know about you, but I don't think I can live here, out in freedom, while other people are prisoners, struggling in the depths of darkness. I'm tired of this, Henri." She walked up to him and put her hands on his chest. "I like you. I really do. And, who knows, if things were better, we might find our way toward more than liking. But I can't; I refuse to go there surrounded by all this mess."

"Why can't I go?" he asked, his voice tiny and pleading.

"Because I need you to stay here and keep my family safe."

"And who keep you safe?"

Caden glanced toward Cate and her brothers. "We'll keep each other safe."

"Okay, enough worrying; let's go," Cate said, patting Henri's shoulder as she passed him. "Don't worry, big guy. Like she said, we'll keep each other safe."

As she entered the kitchen, she slung a stash on one shoulder and gave the brute back his gun. "No point in bringing this without bullets."

"Not easy to shoot, either," Caden said, stepping away from him.

"I give you until tomorrow night. Then I come find you. Keme and me get you back." He glanced about for the other brute, but the man had disappeared.

"Can't stop you," Caden said as she gathered some supplies. "Just make sure the others are okay. That's all I ask." Without another word, she left quickly as though she feared her courage would fail if she stayed near Henri for a moment longer.

Cate caught up with her while Teddy and Jolon came up behind them.

"You okay?" Cate asked, falling into step with her friend.

"About as good as everything usually is," Caden answered with a sniffle. She wiped her nose her gaze turned away.

"Like the haircut," Cate offered in a flimsy attempt at distracting her.

The other girl smiled and heaved a heavy sigh. "Thanks. Oh, I need a break from all this."

"Maybe you should stay. The three of us can deal with this."

"Yeah, we're a dangerous trio," Jolon said, prancing past and waving a stick. "We can deal with whatever comes up." He stopped, puffing. "Okay, maybe after a quick break to catch my breath."

"You are so weird," Cate said, and Caden laughed.

"Thank you. I've decided that's a compliment."

"I meant it as one."

He bowed. "Thing is, I'm better than I used to be. I think it's all this outdoor life. I'm only tired now. Four hours sleep after last night's adventure. Not enough to keep a person going."

"So what are we doing? Do we go in the same way we have the last few times or what?" Caden asked.

Teddy scrunched his features, nibbling his lip. "Belinda has probably doubled the guards on the window entrance and is probably searching the area near the pharmacy. I think we should go back the same way Cate and Jol found."

"The scrounger tunnel just off the square?" Caden asked.

"I think we should wing it like we have since this all began," Jolon suggested. "It's worked really well for us so far. Why break a bad habit with planning?"

Cate flicked him on the back. "Yeah, why mess with imperfection?"

"That's not quite what I was thinking, but it's a start," Teddy said.

"Fine. Makes sense." Caden hid a grin behind tight lips, and Cate nudged her.

Once the stars were bright dots in the sky, they ventured back into Uppercity. The sliver of a moon barely lit the way and made finding the opening difficult. Jolon and Caden slipped in the passage first while Cate and Teddy came up behind.

Teddy's foot ached more than he liked, and he suspected he strained the joint on the last excursion. As he passed the entrance, he brushed against large purple flowers dripping off the side of the building. A spicy perfume drifted on the wind. He sighed inside as doubt and fear played with his courage.

Beyond the glass door and the trashed alcove was the deep, dark, overwhelming hole, which waited for him, pulling him back into the abyss of Undercity.

"I'm so tired," he muttered more to himself than anyone else.

Cate passed him her handlight. "Now is not the time to fall apart, old man. Everyone's tired."

"Yeah. I just... I don't want to lose...." Words failed as he thought of the risk they were about to take.

She grasped his hand. "Me either."

Jolon stuck his head out from around a corner. "You two coming or going for a picnic?"

"Right behind you, Jol." He squeezed her hand and shone his light down the tunnel, pushing a hole into the black.

"This late at night most everyone should be asleep," Caden said as they caught up with her at the entrance to the inner area. She inched the door open and peered through the crack. "Looks clear. Let's go."

A faint glow from a track running the length of the hallway near the ceiling lit the way. An uncomfortable silence sent irritating shivers all the way down the back of Teddy's neck. He rolled his shoulders to relieve the tension.

They crept along, keeping their footsteps quiet. When they reached the square, they paused, searching for signs of loitering Upperlords, brutes, or servants. After what felt like half his life, Caden nudged him, and he nodded.

Wary of being caught, they kept to the edge, following along the wall and slipping quickly past passage openings until they reached the doorway, which led to Belinda's tower, the pharmacy, and the dungeon.

Jolon took the lead and brought them to the stairwell where he had spent the afternoon waiting for Dorkas two days ago. Careful and quiet, they snuck down the flight of stairs to the landing above the level where two brutes guarded the door. As silent as they were, every movement seemed to echo off the cement walls.

The guards at the door shifted a little as though talking to each other as they had been before, but they gave no sign of alarm. It was as though the brutes hadn't noticed them. Something about their body language seemed strange. Their posture seemed very deliberate, as though intentionally keeping themselves from looking up. As though...

Teddy's heart played double time in his chest as a nagging fear surfaced. It was a trap. Somehow, they were expected.

He exchanged a glance with the others and saw the same realization mirrored in their eyes.

"Shit," Caden mouthed and moved to retreat, but was too late.

Lights spilled in from everywhere as booted feet pounded on the steps above them. At the same time the guards below charged toward them.

"Run!" Teddy yelled, bolting back the way they came. He swung his handlight and clipped one on the head as the guy came into range. Cate sent out a kick that caught him in the gut and the guard tumbled back onto his partner. Without looking back, they burst through the door to the main passage.

"Split up," yelled Jolon as he grabbed Caden's hand and took off in a different direction.

Teddy grasped Cate's arm and bolted in the opposite direction, dragging her along. His injured ankle burned at the abuse, but he didn't stop or slow. They had to find a place to hide. He stumbled and Cate caught him.

"Come on. They're right behind us," she said, wrapping an arm around him.

Together, they rushed ahead as best as they could but came to an abrupt halt as two more brutes blocked the way. Gasping and limping, Teddy put his back against the wall, pulling Cate beside him. Dorkas stepped around one of the brutes, a triumphant, twisted grin on his ugly lips. The creeper swaggered before them, nodding, his tongue flicking out over his lips.

"Ah, huh. Figured it was you bunch." The slug stepped in close to Teddy, his breath foul. "Always gotta play the hero. Such an idiot."

"At least, I'm not scum," Teddy said, spitting at him.

Pain shot through Teddy's jaw as Dorkas backhanded him across the face. "Yes, yes you are," he hissed, spittle spraying everywhere. "Well, this is it. They have plans for you."

He thumped himself on the chest. "I figured you out, you know. It was me. You all think of me as less than rat crap." The flick of his hand caught Teddy on the cheek.

"You and those pathetic books. It was me who realized you saved your pa." He spat as though the word poisoned him. "And I figured out you would want to help him. Yes, Belinda realized her waste of a sister would tell you about the pharmacy, but I, I was the one who devised the plan to catch you all. We put it all together."

His grin widened as he turned, his watery eyes narrowing. "Tell me, how's your new friend?"

Teddy's stomach churned, and bile crept up his throat. "No."

The creeper laughed. "Yep. I was supposed to get rid of the rest of your pathetic followers. Then I figured you would come back for the useless garbage. We're so sick of having you and your pitiful bunch popping up and messing with everything. So we let you have the medicine." He shrugged, and Teddy wanted to rip his arms off. "No reason not to. Nothing you do can save your pa. He's gonna die."

Heedless of the guards, Teddy lunged for him, his eyes locked on the scum's neck. One of the guards clipped him on the head, sending him to his knees as sparks clouded his vision.

"Don't hurt him too bad," Dorkas ordered as he hid behind the nearest brute. "We have plans for him." He pulled Teddy's head up by his hair. "Said you were mine, pretty boy. Now, I get to sell you to the highest bidder."

Caden tried to keep up with Jolon, but her side ached with stabbing stitches, and her knees protested the abuse. Despite the pain, she and Jolon wound through so many passages and stairs she lost all sense of direction. At first, the sound of their pursuers followed close with stamping feet and shouts of anger, but gradually they fell back until she heard nothing, but the rhythm of their own panicked steps.

Her brother threw open a side door, and they rushed into an empty room no bigger than a closet. Empty metal shelves lined one wall, and some kind of bulky machine stood against the other.

Gasping, she helped Jolon push the machine in front of the door to block it.

"It's on wheels," he said, leaning against the side. "This isn't going to hold."

She sunk to the floor, her hands on her temples as her brain throbbed. "Don't care at the moment. Need to rest." Flicks of light filled her vision, and she blinked to clear them. "Oh, bloody, pathetic dung-brains. How could we not suspect? We... we just walked in here like we had everything under control."

"Yeah, not our brightest moment." He sagged to the floor, his eyes bright. "Do you think the others got away?"

"Hope so," she said and crawled beside him, grasping his hand and leaning her head against the machine.

"What do we do now?"

Staring at the tiled ceiling, she pulled her knees up. "Rest. Wait and sneak out in a while. See if we can get back to the house." Tears and fear constricted her throat, making it almost impossible to swallow. "Henri was right. We should never have gone without him."

"Keme didn't argue."

"What?" she asked, snapping her head around to look at him.

"Henri's friend, Keme, he didn't argue when we were going to go back without him," he said, his face buried in his hands.

"So?"

He scrubbed his head and groaned. "So, I don't know. My brain is messing with me."

"We need to go back to the stairwell and see what's behind that door," she said, getting to her knees.

Jolon stared at her with bug eyes, and she almost doubted her conviction.

"No, we do. This is our chance. If we slip back, they won't be expecting that. Dorkas thinks we're going to try and hide, escape." She eyed him expectantly, hoping he would agree.

"Instead, we're sneaking back to free the others," he said though his face didn't agree. "What if it's another trick? Or there's nothing behind that door?"

"Then we'll find out," she said though the possibility did cross her mind. Unfortunately, she had no way of confirming the other prisoners were being held somewhere behind that door except her own nagging intuition.

"What about Teddy and Cate?"

"They're fine," she said, as she sat back and scuffed the ground with her boot. "They're both clever and resourceful. We'll probably run into them sneaking back too."

As he emitted a low groan, he rolled his eyes. "Ah, you people are annoying. All these heroes; I want a new family."

She snickered and nudged him. "Okay, hero."

They waited another hour, during which Caden's stomach tied in knots from hunger. "Why does a person get hungry at night?" She rubbed her abdomen to relieve the cramps.

"I get hungry most times. I hold no preference for night or day," he said with a sigh.

"Let's go," she said and smacked his leg.

Worn-out and famished as they were, they shoved the machine aside. Caden crouched low on the floor while Jolon edged the door opened to check the hallway. As she held her breath, she crawled out on her hands and knees, ready to bolt back into the room at the slightest noise. Keeping low to the ground, they crept back down the hall.

"Do you know which way to go?" Jolon asked, inching along behind her.

She halted, her knees sore despite the cushioning of the worn grey carpet. "I... huh."

The passages branched off in all directions with little evidence to show which way they travelled.

"You remember which way we came?" she asked.

"Perfect." He scooted past her and headed down the hall to the left.

"Wha... where are you going?" she asked, hurrying to catch up.

"I'm picking. Is it the right way? Haven't a clue, but we're moving."

Chapter 13

Uncomfortable and in pain, Cate tried to shift her legs, but with her arms twisted behind her back and bound tight to her ankles, the ropes only dug into her flesh. The fog of unsettled sleep muddled her brain. She wriggled around, searching for Teddy while trying to keep her face off the disgusting, stinking carpet beneath her. The room was so dark she wasn't certain he was still with her.

"Teddy? Where'd you go?" An itch irritated her dry throat, making her cough.

"I'm here."

"Where?" Straining, she managed to get onto her haunches. The position still wasn't comfortable, but the tension lessened in her neck and shoulders.

"Right here. You all right?" His voice came closer, and she barely discerned movement as he inched toward her.

"Can't believe I fell asleep," she said as they wiggled close and leaned into each other. The warmth of his body soothed her.

"Exhaustion will do that... and the dark... no air. It's amazing we're conscious at all."

"Dorkas is going to sell us, isn't he?" A shudder made her arms twitch as flashes of memories crowded in her brain.

"I've been close to this before. Years ago. I remember pieces of it like some of those puzzles we'd find... glimpses of pictures. Creepers would scan the halls of the Nest every day—poking, prodding, stripping people, children down and examining them as though they were parcels, a commodity. One creeper with long teeth and scars down his neck had these hands, grey, claw-like hands. Black and green streaked his thick nails, which were sharp and scraped the skin." Every muscle in her body clenched and vibrated with revulsion at the memory.

"I was of poor quality, but worth a few credits if they played me up right and found the right sucker."

Teddy leaned his head against hers, his lips brushing her forehead. "Those asinine twits are the ones who are poor quality, the worst quality. Scum that scum wouldn't want around."

"Ah, my legs are falling asleep. How are we getting out of this?" she asked, suddenly overwhelmed with the desire to kiss him again. Self-conscious, she shrugged him off and squirmed about. "Can you reach my ropes?" Her fingers caught on his, but the bonds were a mess of knots and flesh.

"I... uh, ow. No, that's not.... "

"Here, just move, ah, hey. Careful," she said as the rope dug into her wrist.

"This isn't going to work. I can't... crap, these are tight. Can't figure out which are my fingers and which are yours."

After several moments of struggling, they gave up, breathless and sore. Exhausted, they rested against each other again, and the silence of the room made her head ache.

"They can't just leave us here, can they?"

Teddy sagged against the wall. "They can do whatever they want."

"Perfect." Cate stared at the floor, the shadowy blotches in the cement making aimless patterns in her brain.

"Come on, I'll try your ropes again." As he squirmed over, she wrenched herself around.

"Even if we get free, how do we get out of here?" she asked, trying to help him free her bonds.

"We'll figure it out," he grunted. "Ahh, these things are tight. Wait, I think... yeah... something gave way."

The ropes around her wrists loosened and her heartbeat picked up. "Yeah, I can move my hand. You've got it," she exclaimed as the bonds relaxed more. Determined to escape, she wriggled and squished her hands until one came free. "Yes." With swift fingers, she released her other hand and her feet.

"Turn around. I'll..." she began but froze as she heard the thumping of approaching footsteps in the hall. At the sound of the handle jiggling, her breath caught in her chest.

"Get out," Teddy hissed, and she glanced about the dark room.

"Where? There's nothing in here, not even a closet."

"Hide behind the door. When they come in, you slip out."

"That's not gonna...."

"It's worth a try. Go."

"And leave you, perfect," she muttered and dashed behind the door just as it opened. Light flooded in, blinding her momentarily.

As Dorkas and a brute entered, Teddy threw himself at them, taking out the creeper at the knees. While they scuffled, Cate took her chance and darted out the door, running down the hall as fast as she could.

Caden pressed flat against the wall as three brutes tromped by an adjoining hallway. As they disappeared around a corner, she and Jolon slipped out and hurried down the opposite direction.

"Jol, you've been dragging me all over. Are you sure we are going in the right direction?"

His face scrunched up in frustration. "Yes, yes. I'm good at directions. I am. This is looking familiar." He pulled at her arm. "It does, doesn't it? Right?"

Exasperated, she slapped his fingers. "Are you panicking?"

"No, yes, maybe." He rubbed his hands against his thighs. "I am so done with all this sneaking about. When this is all over, I am never going inside anywhere."

"What? You're going to live outside in the rain, and whatever else nature throws at you? That makes sense." With a deep breath, she pushed on the silver bar on the nearest door and peeked through, listening for signs of life. "All is clear."

They slipped in and kept their steps quiet as they went down, senses straining, but they encountered no one.

"This is it," Jolon said, his whispered voice rising to squeaking rat level with excitement.

"This is what?" she asked as he pressed her against the rail to peer down the stairwell.

"Yep, this the right staircase. Two levels down and we're back at the door."

Sceptical, she raised an eyebrow. "Jol, we've been up and down all over. How can you tell?"

He pointed at a squiggle of a water stain in the shape of two snakes fighting. "I remember that from when I had to watch and wait for Dorkas the last time. I spent five hours alternating between staring at the guards and the wall. This is where we want to be."

"Because of a water stain on the wall."

Her brother nodded, his chest deflating with relief. "Because of that water stain on the wall."

Unconvinced, she rubbed at her nose, fidgeting with indecision. "Right. Now what?"

The proud expression on his face dulled. "Well." He peered over the rail again. "I can't see any guards. Either they are all searching for us, or Belinda doesn't feel the need to guard anyone anymore."

"Or nothing's there. Or they don't have to guard anyone anymore because they're all dead," she said with a sinking knot in her bowels.

"Yeah," he said, his chin wobbling and eyes glistening.

After hesitating for only a moment, she crept down the stairs before her resolve gave way. Jolon kept close, fear vibrating off him and mixing with her own apprehension. Her breath almost solidified in her chest as they approached the door, her senses taunt as she expected to get caught at any moment. Hand shaking, she pushed the bar across the door, hesitating as the metal clanked.

"What if we go in, and we can't get out? What if we're wrong, and there's no one down there? What if there's nothing but dead?" he asked as her fingers locked up.

"Jol!" she hissed through gritted teeth. "Shut up."

After a sharp inhale, she pushed the door open far enough to slip through. The hall was dim with only a few pathetic lights lining the ceiling. Jolon rushed in behind her, and she checked the handle before letting the door close quietly.

"It's not locked, so getting out shouldn't be a problem."

"Yeah, unless the guards come back and block the way."

"Do you want to wait here in case they do?" she said with a hiss.

Mouth working like one of Jemma's fish, he backed against the wall, pressing a hand against his chest. "Me? Alone? Here? No. I'm a coward, a very reluctant hero. Leave me here by myself, and I'll lose all courage. Bravery will seep out of the soles of my feet, and they'll be so light I'll run."

"You are not. If you were a coward, you wouldn't be here," she said, grabbing his shirt and pulling him inside.

"Oh, no, no. Given a better alternative, I would be almost anywhere but here," he insisted, waving his hands in protest.

"Come on. Let's see where this leads. You go first, and I'll watch your back. That way, you can't run." She chuckled under her breath as he slumped his shoulders in dramatic defeat and lumbered off in front of her.

"Fine, but I warn you my courage meter is very low."

As they followed the hall, the ground slanted downward as though the building sagged in its foundation. Jolon pulled out his handlight as the passage dissolved into darkness. The walls and ceiling disappeared, leaving them on a narrow ledge with a cavern of empty black all around.

"How is this place even staying up?" Caden asked, keeping her voice low, fearing any loud noise would send the precarious path crumbling into nothing.

"How is this place staying up? How about the building above us?" Jolon said, his voice shaking. "This is ridiculous. There can't be anyone down here."

"Shh," Caden said as she grasped his arm and halted. "Listen. I heard something."

As they froze in their steps, she strained to hear the strange murmur she thought she heard before. "There, what is that? Sounds like voices."

"Or ghosts, or ratdogs, or some twisted monster contemplating how to have us for a snack."

Ignoring him, she took out her own light and shone the beam on the cement path with crumbling, jagged edges and bits of gravel made the surface slippery. She stayed close to Jolon as they continued toward the sound. The voices became distinguishable, and her light caught the side of a wider ledge.

"This is horrible. I can't, I can't...." Words stuck in her throat, and she sputtered to a stop as her beam revealed rows of people slumped along the wall. With a shaking hand, she moved the light across the prisoners, exposing the faces of friends: drawn, tortured, and dying.

"Cad, we gotta help," Jolon said as he darted past her and dropped to his knees by one of the hostages. "Caden, bring your light here. They're chained together. Help me."

Jaw clenched, she worked her feet free of the paralysis keeping her in one spot, and she stumbled over to him. Angry muttering spilled from his lips as he hammered and pulled at their restraints.

"Jo... Jol... Jolon? Caden?"

Someone called from a few people over and Caden nearly collapsed as she recognized the voice.

"Mrs. Fish? Oh, no. Oh, no, no, no." She scrambled to free the woman, tugging at the restraints binding her to her neighbours. Each person had a crude metal cuff bent around one wrist, which ended in a large loop that the Uppers had threaded the heavy cable through. Caden's fingers scraped at the cement, chipping her nails and tearing the soft flesh of her fingertips.

"Don't worry, we'll get you free." Desperate, she brushed at Mrs. Fish's filthy matted hair and fevered cheeks. "I just... we have to...." She hauled on the cable, futilely trying to break the tightly wound metal fibers. "If we get you free, we can get you out. We will... we will...."

"Cad. Stop." Jolon pulled at her and wrapped his arms around her. "It's not working. They're bolted too far into the wall. We need tools."

Frantic, she whipped around, searching for anything to help. Dark streaks of some kind of liquid made a trail down the ledge, ending in a wide rusted door marred with finger-like streaks. "There, the door there; where does it go?"

"The brutes drag people in there." Mrs. Fish's voice cracked, her eyes huge and streaked with red and mouth contorted. "They drag... mmhh-mmh... they...." Chest heaving, she gasped for air.

It took a moment before Caden realized the woman was laughing bitterly.

"They're fattening us up. We're someone's next meal."

Caden shut the words out, cornering all the disgust and horror in the place in her brain where all the rest of the garbage hid. "There may be tools or something we can use in that room."

"Wait. Cad, wait," Jolon said as she rushed to the door and tugged on the handle. The metal screeched liked a wounded cat and sent stabbing shards through her nerves. A disgusting stench of rotting flesh and congealed blood made her gag, and she pulled back, covering her nose and mouth with the collar of her shirt.

Her brother came up beside her, his face partially covered with his own shirt. He shone his light in, his shaking hand making the beam of light twitch.

"Oh, crap, I don't want to go in there."

"Got a better idea?" she asked with annoyance and hope while her own fears worked out an escape plan in her head.

"No," he whispered and stepped into the room.

Cate didn't know where she was going; she only knew stopping was a fatal mistake she didn't intend to make. She bolted down the first turn she found, the angry voices of Dorkas and a brute following her. The sound of rushing footsteps made her legs speed up. Terrified, she turned her head from side to side to see better, searching for some way to go.

A hand touched her arm, and she yelped, beating at the strange appendage while she whirled about to get free.

"Ow, hey, it's me."

Gasping, she stared at Cratchen. "Where'd you come from?"

"Shh." He tugged on her arm and led her through a side room and down another hall, blocking the door with a chair before continuing to a set of stairs. When they were certain they had lost any pursuers, they slowed.

"Was gonna stay away. I was. Was gonna play games with Deb...watch that big round thing in the sky she says is the moon...or explore some of those junked houses nearby."

"But?"

His thin shoulders twitched. "But...ah, whatever."

She gave a soft snicker. "Yeah, whatever, hero. But how'd you get here? How'd you find us?"

"See, that's the curse and blessing of being small. Curse—you guys underestimate me. I followed you. And blessing—the creeper and his brutes didn't notice me. I bolted and hid at the first sign of trouble then followed them when I saw you get caught. I was just about to rescue you with a brilliant plan when you rushed by and spoiled it all."

With quick steps, they slipped through another door, which opened to the market. Crowds of people mingled about, and they melted into the midst of the gathering.

"We have to go back," Cate said, working to keep up with him as they wound around shopping Uppers. "Teddy's back there. We have to free him."

"Yeah, I get that, but how?" He ducked under the arm of a demonstrative Upper animating a loud story.

A couple of creepers cast their gaze her way, and she avoided eye contact. The press of the people made breathing difficult. "We need to find a safe place to think."

"Yeah, but we can't just...."

All his words melted in with the rest of noise as she spied an exit. With a quick dart around a plump Upper, she shoved the door open and plunged into a back hall. A few Underlings glared at her as she stumbled into them, but she ignored their complaints, and they continued on, disappearing through the exit as Cratchen came through.

"Why do I follow you? You always leave me behind," he exclaimed, his features screwed up with disappointment and frustration.

Spent, she leaned against the wall, bending over to calm down while her head threatened to pop off. "Wasn't leaving you. Needed space."

"So we... you guys... you were setup?" the kid asked, fidgeting beside her.

"Yep." With her hands on her sides, she straightened and nodded. "You, you should probably disappear. Any Uppers connect you with us, and you are only going to get trouble."

The kid snorted. "Right. What am I gonna do, go back to the market? Wander outside on my own?" "Trot back to your ma and pretend nothing happened?"

"That's not a horrible idea," she said, tapping her fingers against her cheek in thought.

He glared, his mouth open to protest, but she waved a hand at him.

"No, no. We need help. We need to get back to the house and get Henri."

"What good is he gonna do?" Cratchen asked, his young face seeming many years older.

Her resolve found strength in the plan hatching in her brain. "Come on," she said with a squeeze to his shoulder. She slipped back into the main area and hid in the press of people, weaving back to an exit. Cratchen trailed behind, muttering something she couldn't quite understand.

Once they neared the back hall that led outside, they rushed down the hidden hall and into a full-on rainstorm.

"Ahhh," Cratchen squealed, covering his head with his shirt. "We're gonna melt." His eyes darted around in fear.

Annoyed, she dragged him forward, the rain helping to clear her head. "No, we won't. Don't be so wimpy. Come on. We have to hurry."

Despite the fear and fatigue dragging at her, Caden crept into the stinking, hideous little room off of the ledge. The floor was sticky, but she kept her gaze up, refusing to check what she was stepping in. The handlight illuminated little, casting shadows that spooked her. Bulky blobs she had no wish to identify hung from the ceiling to her left. There was something too familiar about the shapes dangling in the dark.

"Don't look," she warned Jolon, who had stayed by the door. "Just don't. Wait outside and keep watch."

Her brother didn't hesitate or argue but backed out fast.

Determined, she clenched her jaw till her teeth hurt and detached herself from the horror of her surroundings. A couple of shelves lined the wall in front of her. Eyes glued to the contents, she strode over and searched for something to help. Quickly, she rummaged through a pile of tools, ignoring the tint of dark red streaked across some of them. Lightheaded, she paused, grabbing the ledge in front of her. She closed her eyes for a moment and pictured the garden in the backyard of the house where the rest of her family hid.

As her equilibrium returned to normal, she found a rusted crowbar at the back of the bottom shelf. Gaze on the door, she rushed out of the room, trying to wipe the place from her memory.

"Here." She thrust the bar at Jolon. "I'll watch; you see if you can get them free."

Though green and shaking, he handed his light to Mrs. Fish and thrust the crowbar between the cable and the bracket securing it to the wall. With a low groan, he pried and struck at the metal, the sound echoing around the cavern. Cringing, she hoped no one was around to hear them.

"Come on you crappy piece of... rahhgh," he yelped and stumbled backward as the bracket let go with a clang.

Caden put a hand to his back to steady him.

"One down, 'bout a hundred to go," he said, huffing. "This is going to take too long."

"Try breaking the end one," Mrs. Fish grunted as she rubbed at her wrist still caught in an iron bracelet. "Then we can thread the cable through and free everyone quicker."

"She's right." Caden shone her light on the end of the cable looped into the first bracket fastened to the wall.

"Ah, we should have brought Henri," her brother muttered as he thwacked at the loop. "I don't have the muscle for this kind of heroic effort."

Helpless, she kept the light fixed on the wall as he worked. Were the others safe? Confusing emotions crowded in. She needed Henri. Tired of being her own hero, she needed his muscular arms and kind strength. Coughing, she wiped moisture from her cheek. No, it was better to dwell on action not impractical, emotional longings.

"How's it going?" she asked, trying to get a better view of Jolon's progress.

"He's almost got it," answered the guy sitting right beside them, and she realized it was Mrs. Fish's husband. The man leaned away and pulled at the cable. "Come on, people, effort here. Pull."

Those prisoners along the wall, who were physically able, tugged and strained, heaving on the metal rope in hopes of helping.

"Keep pulling," Jolon said, as he struck again and again. Tiny sparks scattered about with each blow. With a great yell, he brought down the crowbar as hard as he could, and the chain gave way, throwing people backward. Breath coming in gasps, her brother sagged to his knees, and she hugged him while the prisoners freed themselves.

Mr. Fish embraced his wife and those around them as people dragged themselves from the floor.

"Thank you," Mrs. Fish said, wrapping Caden in a long hug. "We've lost so many." She glanced toward the little room, visibly shuddering. "We have to get out of here before they come back."

"Right. Jol, give your light to Mr. Fish so he can illuminate the bridge while people cross." She dug in her stash and pulled out a tiny handlight and passed it to one of the Fish's sons. "This one's not too big, but you stay in the centre of the pack and use it to help people see where they're going. I'll go up front with mine. It's the best we've got, so people will have to go slow and careful."

Nobody argued as they formed a ragged line. They were either too afraid to complain or too tired not to try.

"Get the crowbar. We'll probably need it," she said to Mr. Fish as he waited by the edge of the path, his face a crumpled map of pain and resolve.

With grim resolve, she stepped forward onto the narrow bridge, keeping her eyes locked on the bit of solid ground lit up by her narrow beam. One step behind, Mrs. Fish leaned on Jolon while they inched across the cavern. Caden kept her light steady on their trail, hoping no one would fall off, and fearing the return of Dorkas and his brutes.

The strength in her body trickled out of her, making her muscles rubbery and weak. Determined to keep moving, she concentrated on each step, ignoring the gradual decline of her being. All they had to do was get across—one step then another—all they had to do was get across. She forced herself to keep breathing, blocking out all other sounds, her concentration locked on staying upright.

Teddy spent a fitful night slipping in and out of sleep. His body ached from lying on the floor with his hands and feet bound behind him. Almost all the feeling had gone from his limbs, and they throbbed with a burning need for more blood. He wormed around, trying to find relief, but that only brought on painful, pinprick waves as his circulation returned.

Every moment that went by, he expected Dorkas' brutes to return with Cate. Hope grew in him as the time passed and she didn't return. Either she got away or... his thoughts crashed to a halt. No, she was resourceful and smart. If anyone could escape, it was her. She would get help. She would find a way.

Dazed from thirst and hunger, he sunk back against the wall, the moment of hope dwindling. Maybe Dorkas was lying. Why? His brain refused to come up with an answer. No. It made sense. The raid on the pharmacy was too easy—Keme's presence too coincidental.

Still... no. His head throbbed, protesting any more thoughts. Alone in the black, he stared at nothing, hoping his family was safe.

A slice of light cut in, hurting his eyes as the door opened and two brutes entered. Before he could say anything, one guard seized him and threw him over his broad shoulder as though he was nothing, but a sack of garbage.

"Where are... we going?" he managed, forcing the words out as his diaphragm pressed into the guy's shoulder. They didn't answer, and he twisted his head about, trying to discern where they were taking him. All he got was glimpses of dirty grey walls and soiled orange carpet as his vision blurred.

As Cate and Cratchen approached the house, the rain continued to pour in a chilling sheet of water. The journey took longer than before as the weather and the dark made the trail difficult to follow. Several times, they had to backtrack as they wandered off the wrong way. The rain lightened up to a soft mist by the time the house materialized, a dull glow of grey light tinted the cloudy sky.

The imposing figure of Keme lurked on the path to the house, his attention on the rising sun. She paused and hid behind a tree, waiting. The brute's manner seemed agitated as he paced, whacking a thin branch against the bushes.

"What are we doing?" Cratchen asked, huddled behind her, his hand on her arm as he peaked toward the house. "Don't tell me the creepers have found the house?"

Bitter with anger over Keme's deceit, she grasped his shoulder and crouched down. "No. Just one."

"Huh?"

"Nevermind. Look, you slip in through the back and check on everyone. See who's up. If Nuna or her wife is around, send them out front."

"What about the other big guy, Henri? You want him too?"

With a quick glance back, she hesitated. Henri was Keme's friend. Were they working for the Uppers together? It didn't seem likely, but she never was good at trusting anyone.

"No. Not yet. Got a few questions to ask first."

The kid leaned around her his brows drawn together and mouth in a frown as he stared at Keme. "You don't trust him."

She patted his shoulder. "Just go. I'll sort it out."

Cratchen sighed and scooted into the underbrush, disappearing, his movements quiet. Cate straightened, wiping crumbs of soil from her hands. Keme sat on the lower part of a rusted piece of metal half covered in soil and grass. The thwack of the branch cut through the quiet morning as he struck a stick against the side of his seat. She approached with caution, keeping him in her vision and her hands loose and at her side.

The traitor's expression flitted from surprise to guilt as he caught sight of her. He jerked to his feet, his stick at his side. Wary, she kept a safe distance away.

"You're back?" he said, shifting from foot to foot.

His whole demeanour made her want to strike him. "You sound surprised? Things not go as you planned?"

A flush of deep red spread up his thick neck and across his face to the roots of his hair. Eyes locked on her; he tried to force his expression blank and innocent. "I... I don't. What?" His shoulders slumped as the air rushed out of his chest. "I'm glad. Where are the others?"

Knots of anger twisted in her gut. "The others? Does it matter?"

"Cate?"

She turned slightly, catching sight of Jemma as she and Nuna came down the walk with Cratchen behind them. The kid held a metal bar tight in his hands, and she admired his courage.

"Cate, you're back," Nuna said, standing between her and Keme. "Cratchen said the others were still there. What happened?"

"Ask him." She glared at Keme, hating his squirming guilt.

The brute backed away, stumbling against the mound of metal and earth. "Me? I don't... why would I know?"

"Yes, why he know?"

For a moment, she closed her eye at the sound of Henri's voice, her heart fluttering, uncertain of how the other brute would react. She straightened her shoulders, she put as much accusation and hate in her narrowed gaze as she opened her eye. "The Uppers knew we were coming. The pharmacy was a trap. And according to the Dorkas creeper, he was supposed to lead them here after we were caught." A bitter chuckle crept from her throat. "You betrayed us."

"No," Henri said, pushing his way between them. "You wrong. He friend. He wouldn't do that." He stood before the other brute, rocking on his feet as he pushed his hair out of his face. "Right?"

Keme stared at him for a second before crumpling. "Yes, I did," he whispered, his head sinking into his hands. "I'm sorry, Henri."

"No," Henri gasped, stepping back as though the man was contagious. "You wouldn't. Not you."

"Why?" asked Nuna with more kindness than Cate thought he deserved.

Cratchen slipped in beside Cate on the fringe of her sightline. He nodded and winked, his pipe ready. Though touched, she almost laughed at the loyalty of his gesture.

"Well, I didn't know," Keme said, rubbing his hands together.

"You didn't know. You didn't know what?" Cate demanded, pushing aside the wet hair clinging to her cheek.

The brute waved a hand at the trees swaying with the wind and the rumbling clouds darkening the sky. "This. I had no understanding of what you had done. The Upperlords said you were some rebels living on the fringe trying to steal from them. They asked me to follow you, find out where you were hiding, and lead you back to the other prisoners."

Henri stepped forward, his face like crumpled paper. If he was crying, the soft mist of rain hid his tears in a layer of moisture on his cheeks.

"Why? Why you betray me? Why you betray my friends, my family?"

"Henri, I didn't know you were one of them," he said, his hands held out, palms up.

"And that made it all okay?" Cratchen threw in, his disgust dagger-hate in his gaze. "I just met 'em, and I wouldn't do that."

"You knew after," Cate added. "You knew Henri was one of us before you sent the rest of us into that trap."

Defeated, he slumped against the metal lump and shook his head. "I... I've been in that underground cellar for so long. The brutes there, they say we're special, important, guarding the future of our society, but we stay there locked away, unable to see anyone else or go anywhere, but those few halls. I needed to get out, and they said..."

"The Upperlords said they would assign you somewhere else if you helped them." It was Teddy's mother. She wandered in between Nuna and Jemma, her arms wrapped around her tight, and her face creased with sorrow.

Jemma wrapped her arms around Mrs. Peterson's thin shoulders, holding her upright.

"They lie. Uppers always lie," she said and dissolved into tears.

"Tisha?" Nuna called, taking the woman's hand and peering into her bloodshot eyes. "Oh, Tisha."

"He's gone. I tried. I did everythin..." her words dropped off in a choking cry. She buried her head against Jemma's shoulder.

"Oh, no. Oh, my dear. I'm so sorry." Nuna helped Jemma turn her around. "Henri, you deal with this..." she glanced with hate back toward Keme, "mess. Come, Tish. Let's go inside. You need rest."

Numb, Cate stared after them until they disappeared into the house. Her heart beat so hard she could barely breathe. She snatched Keme's stick from the ground and thwacked him hard on the arm.

"You see? You see what they do?" She hit him again and again. "She's right. They lie. They devour and lie. And you let them destroy us."

Henri grabbed her, wrestling the branch from her hands. "Stop. Stop. Not helping. No."

With a desperate scream, she struggled to get out of his grip, kicking at the other brute who did nothing to stop her or protect himself.

"I know, I know," he exclaimed, sliding to the soggy ground, wild grasses clinging to him like chains. "I'm sorry. I'm so sorry."

"Cate, Cate!" Henri forced her to meet his gaze. "Where are others?"

Snuffling, she spat and wiped her face with her soaked sleeve. "I don't know. We all got separated. They caught Teddy and me and stuffed us in this dark room. Dorkas was there. I think they're going to sell him."

"Sell him?"

"Yeah." She kicked Keme again. "I hate you."

"If the Upperlords are planning to sell him, they'll want to use him as an example," Cratchen cut in.

Cate pulled out of Henri's grip. "How?"

"Lately, they've been using the center square by the clock tower," the kid said. "That way both Uppers and Unders can witness the person's disgrace. Since you all escaped, the Uppers have been doing all kinds of weird stuff like that to show their power."

The rain started to pick up again, but Cate didn't care. An idea was forming in her brain. "The center square, it has sky windows, doesn't it?"

Puzzled, the kid tilted his head and drew his brows together. "Yeah, why?"

"Henri, if we can get up to those windows, can you smash them?"

"No," Keme cut in. "You can't."

The expression Henri gave him was pure scorn. "How you know?"

Keme got to his feet, and Cate grabbed her stick again in case he tried anything.

"Think about it. If they didn't break when the meteor and the earthquakes hit, what makes you think they'll break now? The glass they're made of is impossible to break."

He had a point, and she hated that.

"The frames," Henri said.

"What?" she asked.

"The frames weak. They break. Whole building crumbling now. We break frames."

Cate could have kissed him. "Yes. Perfect. We'll take the glass out by the frames. Everything around here is rusting and rotting." She waved a hand toward the house. "This place is barely standing, and it's one of the better places around. We can do this."

"Let's go," Cratchen said, vibrating with excitement.

"No." Cate put a hand on his shoulder. "You stay here with the others."

"No way," he squealed, his cheeks flushing.

"Yes. You've been up all night...."

He crossed his arms in defiance. "So have you."

"Doesn't matter." She knelt beside him. "I need you to stay here and care for the others. I need Henri's help, and I don't trust slimy for anything. Please, Cretch, do this for me."

The kid licked his lips and worked his mouth as though chewing over what she said. "Fine. I'll stay, but you have to promise you'll come back."

With a tolerant grin, she ruffled his drenched hair, sending a spray of water everywhere. "Will do. Now, go round me up some food. I gotta eat something before we go back or I won't make two more steps."

He chuckled and tore off toward the house. Exhausted, Cate forced herself to her feet, her head light from a long night and nothing to keep her going. Her pants and shirt stuck to her body, making movement uncomfortable, but there was no point in changing. The rain continued to pour and did not seem to have any intentions of stopping.

"What we do with him?" Henri asked without sparing a glance toward the other brute.

As she pondered Keme for a moment, he kept his gaze on the ground. Rain soaked him, making him a pitiful sight. The traitor could stay with the others, or go with them. Neither seemed to be a good choice.

"We can't trust him."

Henri's face screwed up like he was chewing sour rat stew. "No."

"Henri." Keme took a step forward, his eyes pleading. "I was going to go back. I was going to tell you the truth and go back to get them."

"Little late," he answered, keeping his face averted. "Tell truth before they go, not after when everyone lost."

If he had punched the traitor, Keme wouldn't look more injured. "Right. Then let me help. Let me go with you and rescue them."

"So you can betray us? Turn us in?" Cate said, resisting the urge to smack him in the head.

"No." He drew his brows together in a pleading line. "You don't trust me, and I don't blame you, but let me prove myself to you."

"Too late," Henri stepped away from the man.

"Henri," Keme said, hands extended with palms up.

"We're wasting time," Cate interjected, tired of debating the issue. "You want to come; we can't stop you unless we tie you up, and I've had enough of that junk." She stepped forward and fixed him with a stern gaze. "But you betray us, and we'll make sure you wish you hadn't. Because the last thing I'll do before I die is make certain, you suffer. I'll take out a knee so you can't walk. I'll take out your eyes so you can't see. I'm small compared to you, but I fight dirty, and I'll make you suffer. Got that?"

"And she don't, I will," Henri added, looming over Keme.

He shrank back from them slightly, his hands trembling. "Okay."

Chapter 14

By the time someone came in and untied Teddy, his limbs were numb and his muscles twisted in painful knots. The drudge cut his bonds and left a bowl of mush, a tin of water, and a bit of a candle barely capable of casting much light.

Once alone, Teddy rubbed his arms and legs until proper function returned, and devoured the mush, ignoring the cold, bland flavour. The cramps in his empty stomach eased, and the parched ache in his throat disappeared as he gulped down the stale water. As much as he wished he could avoid eating the meal in protest, he needed the nourishment more.

Somewhat better, he took the light and wandered the empty room. The place wasn't big, maybe twenty by twenty, and boards covered what had to be a window. After putting his candle down, he tried to pry the wood from the wall, but nothing budged. With a heavy sigh, he relieved himself in a dank corner where water stains crept up the wall.

After walking in endless circles, his candle went out and plunged him in darkness again. Despondent, he sunk to his knees, the concrete cold on his limbs. They were going to leave him there.

No, that made little sense.

Dorkas brought him food. If the creeper was going to hide him away, why not let him starve or shoot him, or dump him in one of the pits?

As the silence echoed in his ears, he hoped Cate got away. She was his best chance at a rescue. Shattered, he lay down and fell into a fitful sleep, drifting in and out as the sensory deprivation dulled his mind.

"Get up."

Teddy blinked then gasped as pain coursed through his ribs. He glared up at Dorkas' smarmy face. For part of a second, he thought about beating the smug bastard, but a beady-eyed brute wrapped his giant hands around Teddy's arms and hauled him off the ground.

"Where are we going?" he asked as the guard all but lifted him through the door.

"Where are we going?" Dorkas repeated in a whining, mocking tone. His laugh grated against the ears.

Brilliant. The creeper was childish as well as a slimy jerk.

"You are going where you should have gone all along." His bulbous eyes slid up and down Teddy with loathing and a strange envied disgust. "Yeah, you'll get a good price. And then your new owners will teach you how to behave." He spat and strode off down the hall.

The brute pushed Teddy along, and he scrambled to catch up with the creeper. All the while, he searched for a quick escape. Dorkas kept a steady pace as they rushed through several entrances and wound their way up to where he started to recognize the area.

The market.

His stomach slid into his bowels. As they approached the more populated sections, the brute clasped Teddy's shoulder in an iron grip, the strong fingers digging into his flesh and muscles.

As Teddy's strength was about to give out, they entered a tiny suite with a worn brown couch and a desk covered in papers. A couple of cupboards, with a sink and a rusted out stove, stood against one wall off to the side. Yellow light streamed down from a fixture hanging from the ceiling. The brute shoved him in the other direction toward a brown door cracked down the middle.

"Get cleaned up. We want you looking good... best price and all."
Dorkas flopped on the couch, the grin on his face disgusting.

Teddy closed the door and leaned against the wood, closing his eyes
in the dim room. After gathering himself together in the silence, he felt
around the wall until he found a switch and flicked it up, hoping for
light. He squinted as a fluorescent bulb above a narrow sink pulsed on,
flickering and humming.

Some clothes lay on a hamper by the sink, and a clean towel hung
from a bar by a corner shower with a glass door. Despite his desire to
escape, he shucked off his clothes and got in the stall. The warm water
poured over him, and he indulged in the sensation, taking the moment
to gain strength.

With any luck, Cate got away and got help. Hopefully, she found
Caden and Jol.

Keme. The brute suckered them in. He didn't question anything.
Why didn't he question any part of it?

Ashamed, he closed his eyes and stuck his face in the moderate
stream. For a moment, he remembered the rain and the first moment
the vital, energizing drops touched his skin. The water drenching him
now was dead, stale... nothing.

Someone hammered on the door, making him jump. "Hurry up.
We've customers waiting."

Hands shaking, he turned off the tap and dried his body. The
clothes they provided were clean but too big by several sizes. He rolled
up the grey trousers and tucked in the faded blue t-shirt. The pants
wouldn't stay up, so he tore off a length of cloth from his old shirt and
fashioned himself a belt. Dorkas banged on the door again as he pulled
his boots back on.

"Get out here, naked or not. Buyers won't care." The door rattled
as he pounded on the wood. "Don't think that lock is gonna protect
you." The knob rattled, breaking as the door flew open. A balding brute
with a crude snake tattoo running up his neck seized Teddy's arm and

dragged him out of the room. The sharp, weasel creeper from the Adult Quarter was waiting with a sick smirk to his purplish lips as he scanned Teddy up and down.

"Eh, yeah." The creeper grasped Teddy's soaking hair and turned his head about. "Skin's pretty good, lacking a little muscle, but decent body."

The thought slipped in his head to bite the creeper's hand and run, but the snake brute tightened his grip as he shoved him into the hall. The weasel and Dorkas went on ahead, cackling to themselves.

He didn't ask where they were going, doubting anyone would tell him. Someone would come. Someone would rescue him—his heart sank into his stomach—if there was anyone left.

Caden and Jolon huddled by the exit leading to the stairs. Behind them, the prisoners lined up, waiting on the narrow path. As she stilled her breathing, she cracked the door open and peered through. No one seemed to be around. After a glance to her brother, who held the pry bar up ready to strike, she shoved the heavy door open as hard as she could in case anyone was behind it.

"Ahhhghhgh," Jolon yelled and charged through, waving the bar about. He whirled around, hopping on his feet. "Ahhhrgh, rarhgh."

"Jol. Shut up. No one's here, but they will be if you keep screaming like that," she said and grabbed his arm.

Huffing, he stared, his eyebrows nearly reaching his hair. "Ah, right."

Mrs. Fish and several others filtered in, blinking in the dim light. "Where do we go from here?"

Caden contemplated their options. "We can't get out through the market."

"No," Jolon said as he sagged against a wall. "What about through the lower tunnels, you know, the way we escaped from the pharmacy?"

She shook her head. "There are too many of us to go that way. The elevator's the only way down. It would take too long." Caden stumbled as the people surged past her and up the stairs. "We need to find Teddy and the others too."

"We'll have to split up," Mrs. Fish said as she leaned against the rail with her son by her side.

Ragged and beaten, no one seemed to have enough strength left to make it up a flight of stairs let alone break free from anyone. The prisoners kept filtering into the stairwell, eager to get away from the dungeon and darkness. The noise echoed up through the floors.

"Someone's gonna notice this," Jolon said as he pressed against the wall, away from the desperate people. "We gotta do something."

Caden pushed her way to Mrs. Fish and grasped the woman's bony hand. "Take whatever route you can and the first window you see, do whatever it takes to break the glass."

The woman's eyes grew wide. "What? No. I know we're desperate, but..."

"Don't worry, outside is safe," Caden said, cutting her off. "Ma is out there right now with Pa and Nuna. They are outside living in the wild. You can go outside. It's our best bet. If we can get out, we will survive this."

Mrs. Fish sunk into herself, her starved body shaking. "I... I don't..."

"You sure about this?" her son asked as he held his mother.

After years of hiding from people due to constant pain and fear, Caden realized she never learned his name. With a quick breath, she tapped into a courage she never knew she had and met his gaze.

"Yes, you can. We've been outside. It's safe." She snatched the crowbar from Jolon and passed it to him. "At least, it's safer than in here. The more people we get outside, the quicker we can all be free. If you find a door or a crack in the wall, go. Whatever you have to do, get out of Uppercity."

"What will you do?" Mrs. Fish asked, her fingers tightening around Caden's.

"We're going to find Teddy and Cate," she said with a nod toward Jolon. "We got separated searching for you all."

Angry shouting erupted above them, and the crowd surged.

"We can't control them," her brother said, grabbing her arm. "Let's go. They're on their own now."

For a moment, she hesitated, holding Mrs. Fish's gaze, but the woman gave her a firm smile and headed up the stairs.

"You heard them. Let's go, people."

Jolon kept a hand on her as Caden worked her way through the prisoners, heading up and away from the crowd. They paused by an upper window, the rain pounding against the glass. An aching cramp worked across her abdomen, and she pressed a hand to her side.

Her brother tapped against the windowpane. "Solid. Take a lot to break it."

"What are you thinking?" she asked as she wiped strands of cobwebs from her face.

"Liked your idea, break the glass," he said with a shrug. "I figure if we break as many windows as we can, open as many doors as possible, the Uppers will be so busy panicking, we can get out of this dump."

"Like that," she said with a grin and gestured to the nearest door. "Let's see where this leads." As she pushed the bar, she took a quick look before entering the empty hall.

"We should head for the market. That's where most of the people are. If we want to make a mess, that's the best place to go."

Cate kept up with Henri, who charged ahead without a single glance for Keme. The other brute scrambled along behind them, his eyes more on his friend than where his feet were going. Morning shadows grew short by the time they reached the buildings of Uppercity. The small meal of rice and fish she had gulped down before they left was gone, and a weakness from lack of sleep tugged at her.

Her breath came in quick gasps as she stared at the filthy grey walls before her, trying to find a way onto the roof.

"It's not too far," Henri said, gesturing toward the rim of the roof two levels above them.

"What do you plan to do, jump?" she asked with a doubtful frown. "That's quite a distance even for you."

"Is there no other place closer?" Keme asked, joining them.

After a moment's silence, Cate realized Henri had no intentions of acknowledging the other brute's existence.

"No. Well, not that we know of, but we don't have the luxury of time to explore further."

"What about that ladder up there?" He pointed toward a run of six metal rungs, which ran down from the top of the roof. "If we found a way to reach it, we could use it to get on the top."

Wiping the rain from her forehead, she scanned the area, searching for something to help. Much of what was left hid in tall grass and under rubble, but there were piles of broken walls and cinderblocks, which might serve them.

"Hey, this place has lots of stuff laying about. What if we piled it up against the wall underneath? Made a ramp or something we can climb easier?" she said to Henri, who seemed caught between wanting to help and wanting to hate.

Keme dragged a piece of wall out from the earth, wet mud and grass slipping off to the ground. "Good idea."

Jaw tight, Henri clenched his hands as though trying to decide whether or not to punch the other brute.

Cate smacked him on the shoulder. "Come on, bulky. Put those muscles to good use." With the persistent rain soaking her through, she broke a dead branch from a tree and whacked at the underbrush. "There's a bench over here. If you two muscle boys work together, we can put it to better use."

Wary of each other, they hauled on the cement seat. The rusted bolts that once held it to the ground broke clean away. Together, the two men dragged the bench out of the bushes. After a short while, they found enough junk to create a good pile though Henri grumbled and Keme twitched like he was about to fall apart.

Henri climbed on top and jumped, grasping the bottom rung. The rails creaked with rust and wear but held. He braced his feet against the wall and inched up the slick brick. One side of the ladder twisted and gave way. With a loud groan, he lunged for the rim of the roof as the metal collapsed.

Cate gasped and held her breath as he dangled for a moment before working his way over the edge. He disappeared, and she waited, keeping her distance from Keme, but the brute kept his gaze on the place where Henri disappeared.

"Hen? You alive up there?" she called, hoping for a quick answer.

The man's broad face appeared over the edge. "Yeah, barely."

Keme climbed on top of the pile of rubble. "Cate, climb on me, and I'll boost you up. Henri can pull you the rest of the way."

Despite the urgency of the situation, she hesitated.

Eyes pleading, he grumbled and pushed wet strands of hair from his face. "I promise this is no trick. I absolutely promise on my life. If I drop you or anything, Henri can crush me or something just as horrible."

"Fine," she said at last and climbed to him, the debris shifting under her feet.

He caught her wrist and helped her onto his knee. From there, she grasped his hands and pushed herself up onto his shoulders. Pressing close to the wall, she wobbled as she let him go and slid her hands up toward Henri.

"A little further," Henri grunted, and she stretched to her toes, precariously shifting on Keme's shoulders.

As Keme grasped her legs to steady her, she caught Henri's hand. The brute held tight though their hold was tentative due to the wetness of their skin. Keme thrust her upward, her chest and stomach scraping against the cement. Muscles straining, she let Henri haul her over the edge and onto the roof, her arms aching in their sockets.

Sore and shaking, she collapsed against the low wall running around the edge of the building. "Well, we're up. Now what?"

Henri stood gazing out over the roof with his feet apart and hands on his hips like some hero about to conquer the world. "We find sky windows."

"Right," she said with an inward groan over his dramatic tone. "What about Keme?" she asked, glancing over the side to where the brute stood gazing about him and waiting.

Henri waved a dismissive hand. "Eh. We better without him." He picked his way around broken branches and large metal boxes.

Despite the ache in her back, she followed him. "Um, won't we need him? He does have a good supply of muscles, which might come in handy."

"No. He no good. He lie. They hurt because he lie."

She couldn't argue with that. "Still, he made a mistake...."

"No!" He whirled around, his hand slicing through the air to end the discussion. "We go. We save."

With one more glance back, she trailed after him in silence. Parts of the roof were damaged by the years of neglect and water pooled deep in many spots. The wind picked up, throwing rain at her and obscuring her already limited vision.

"Henri," she shouted to get her voice above the scream of the storm. "You see anything?" She stumbled over a coil of wires and grabbed his arm to steady herself.

"Don't know what looking for."

A crack of white light cut through the sky with a tremendous crash, and she screamed. "Scab of an ass-biter, what was that?"

"Keep going," Henri said though he shook visibly. "Has to be here somewhere."

Limbs heavy with fatigue, she climbed over a pile of rusted pipes, searching for something that might be the windows. Her shirt snagged on a shard of metal. The sharp, jagged edge cut into her arm, and blood trickled down her bicep. She tore off her sleeve and did her best to tie the scrap of material around the wound.

"Here," shouted Henri, beckoning to her a short distance away.

Drained of most of her strength, she stumbled over to him. A layer of mud covered a structure, which came to just above her knee and stretched out across a third of the middle of the roof. The driving rain made rivers of silt, which revealed tinted panes of glass.

"Well, they're sky windows. Question is, are they the right ones?"

Henri picked up a broken pipe and brought the metal down hard against the glass. "Don't matter. Break anyway."

"Aim for the frames," she said as she found her own piece and struck. Her aching arms shook at the impact, but she kept going, Henri's drive and determination pushing them both along.

Teddy stumbled as the brute shoved him to the floor in front of the clock tower. Rain beat hard on the windows above, adding to the noise of the gathering crowd. Belinda and her cohorts stood a few steps away, their brutes keeping track of the extra people. The Upperlord moved in front of him and forced him to face her.

"All this trouble. You are not worth all this trouble," she said with a scornful twist to her lips. "I had hoped to catch more of you, but you'll do for a start. Make back some of what I've lost."

"You've lost?" Teddy said, jerking his jaw from her grip. "What have you lost? Nothing in compari...."

He bit his tongue as she struck him, cutting off his words.

"You will learn your place. Now, let's get on with this. We'll find the rest of your pathetic family later."

"No you won't," he said as she turned away.

She paused in her next step. "Don't be tiring. There is nowhere anyone can hide we can't get to."

"They're outside."

A rumbling gasp rippled through the crowd, and he grinned inside but schooled his features to be as cold and severe as hers.

"Oh, don't bore me with that old tale." Though her tone feigned disbelief, the twitch in her hands gave her away. She turned back toward him, crossing her arms over her chest. "No one is outside."

He laughed and spoke louder, so everyone heard him. "Yes, they are. They are living out in the sunshine and rain, thriving, breathing fresh air and everything."

"No," gasped one of her cohorts and the others threw in their comments of horrified disbelief.

The crowd surged with restless worry. Teddy got to his feet, pushing his advantage.

"They are out there living their lives." He stabbed a finger toward the mud-covered sky windows. "They are healing and growing, and out of your grasp. Free."

"Quiet," she yelled and struck him again, but he didn't care.

"Let it go, Belinda." He wiped the blood from his lip. "You've lost. No one needs you anymore. Not to live. We're free." He raised his hands and gestured to the growing crowd. "We're all free."

"It's true," said Caden as she and Jolon stepped forward, and he wasn't certain if he was glad to see them or not. "It's all true. We've been outside too."

One of Belinda's servants wormed through the crowd and whispered in the Upperlord's ear. She shoved him away. "Lies!"

"It's true," the grovelling man said, backing away. "They're breaking every window they can find."

Right at that moment, a tremendous crash drowned out any protests as the windows above gave way. Glass, metal, and rubble showered down along with the driving rain. Teddy scrambled for cover. The wind drove in, scattering the people.

He stumbled as Dorkas seized his leg. "No, you don't. You are not getting away this time."

Teddy kicked at the creeper and twisted to escape. Another shower of debris fell, and he barely missed getting impaled by a piece of metal. Rain drenched the ground, sending people into a frantic scramble. Panicked, terrified Underlings and Upperlords screeched and wailed, throwing themselves about.

Dorkas swung a pipe at him, but he blocked it with a piece of jagged wood.

"You and your family, you ruined everything," he screamed, his eyes wild as he stood over Teddy, his face distorted by abject anger.

"Teddy!" Caden appeared at his side with Jolon nearby. She caught the creeper in the knee with a twisted piece of metal.

As he bellowed in pain, he collapsed onto the other knee. Teddy took his chance, thwacking his attacker up the side of the head. Dazed, Dorkas stumbled and fell back as more of the ceiling gave way.

Teddy threw a protective arm over his head and rolled away, taking cover at the base of the clock. Pain shot through him as a hand grasped his injured ankle, dragging him away from the crowd.

"Stop struggling," Jolon yelped as Teddy kicked at him. He seized Teddy's hand and hauled him up. "Come on. Let's get out of here before the whole place gives way."

Caden limped past them, urging them on. "This way."

They weaved through the people, dodging brutes and frantic Uppers. Nobody chased after them; they were too concerned with their own survival. Where Belinda and her followers went, he couldn't tell.

A man in a black robe stumbled against a post, his skin soaked and eyes despondent. "Ah, dying, I'm dying. It's burning me."

Jolon smacked him on the side of the head as they went by. "It's only rain; you dope. Get up and do something useful."

Whether he listened or not, they didn't wait to find out. They ran down the halls and through the Upper square. Finally, they escaped into the back passage that led to freedom. They stumbled through the door and into the wild storm raging outside. Despite their fatigue, they kept going, desperate to get away from Uppercity.

Cate stumbled backward when the glass frame gave way. Both she and Henri paused as a loud crack emanated from the structure. The surface beneath her feet wobbled, and she crept toward the edge of the roof.

"I think we set off something. I don't think this will hold anymore." One window wobbled and broke away from the frame as the side of the structure crumbled.

"Building bad." He threw his pipe at the weakest point. Rain gushed in, adding to the damage they started. The roof buckled and pools of water rushed toward the growing hole.

"Yeah." She tugged on his arm. "Let's find safer ground before...." The rumbling of the sky drowned out her words, and they stumbled away as the rest of the windows gave way.

They gave up being careful and ran back the way they came.

Running, Caden was tired of running. Her legs no longer wanted to work, and the pounding rain just added to her fatigue. They were free of Uppercity, but many others followed them out of the dying city. Fear and panic made people unpredictable, and they crashed through the trees with little regard for those around them.

Caden held onto Teddy and Jolon as they made their way back to Ma and their house. She slipped on the wet grass and fell hard against the stone path. For a moment, she lay still, trying to gather the strength to keep going. Her body had enough. No amount of adrenaline could free her from the innate physical weakness in her muscles. Black dots obscured her vision, and she closed her eyes, willing the dizziness to go away.

Someone scooped her off the ground. Dazed, she flicked open her eyelids to see the worried face of Henri gazing down at her. "Where'd you come from?"

"Sky." His partial grin puzzled her.

"Ah," she said, sinking against his chest and taking comfort in his arms. "Take me home, muscles. I'm done."

Chapter 15

Teddy sat in the bright sunlight, enjoying the warmth on his back. He placed a small bouquet of flowers on his father's grave as Cate joined him.

"Cad and Jol said you were out here. I'm sorry you didn't get to say goodbye." The words came out awkward though he knew they were well meant.

He slipped his hand into hers. "That would have been nice."

"I like the marker," she said, gesturing to the bronze statue of a horse they placed at the head of the grave.

"Cratchen found it when scrounging one of the nearby shops. Ma thought it was perfect." He dusted the grass off his pants as he stood and turned back to the house. "You're back from your hunt early. Went well, I hope. Fresh meat would be good."

"Just got back. Jemma brought me to this meadow and between us we trapped a deer. She's brilliant at thinking up traps. Ma and Nuna are carving the carcass up in that garage area." She linked her arm in his. "The place is coming together nicely."

"Yeah. Henri fixed the loose roof tiles, and we spent yesterday replacing old boards with new ones we scrounged from some of the more dilapidated houses."

They went through a small metal gate and wandered down a street dappled in leaf-shadows and sunlight.

"Mrs. Fish like her new home?"

He chuckled. "Oh, yes. She and her brood are turning it into a palace. The rest of the tower people who survived have either returned to the tower or moved on." He shrugged. "Most Uppers and Underlings have."

"Any sign of Keme? He disappeared after he helped Henri and I off the roof."

"No, though I think Henri feels bad about it. Cad says she catches him staring out the window sometimes. Apparently, he was thinking of going to search for him."

"Won't happen. He won't leave her for anyone. What about Belinda and her crew? Any sign of them?"

Pausing, he turned back and gazed toward the ugly structure that once was Undercity. "Well, according to Henri's sentries, they have holed themselves up in what's left of the city, keeping to the greenhouses and surrounding buildings. The market is gone. The whole building collapsed and slid into the pits."

"Sad. Why would anyone want to seal themselves away from all this if they didn't have to?"

"They liked what they had, I guess."

"Was only a matter of time, then."

He gazed at her, smiling at the light in her green eye. "What was?"

"The destruction of Uppercity. It was inevitable."

"Yeah," he said with a slow exhale. He brushed a curl from her face and kissed her soft lips, lingering in her embrace as a warm wind curled around them.

Please, give a Review.

Thanks for joining in on the Undercity adventure. Reviews are the lifeblood of authors. They help indie authors show up better online and allow us to write more books for you. If you enjoyed this story, please leave a review on the site you bought this book from. Thank you so much.

Connect with us at:
www.juliettestudios.com
Twitter: @juliettestudios
Instagram: @juliettestudios
Facebook: Juliette Studios

About the Author

Kris Moger – The words and ideas.

Like many creative people, Kris Moger doesn't like writing bios, but she got talked into it this time. On an average day, she likes to write, draw, and daydream. On most days, she cleans house, gets distracted, and procrastinates. She has created stories since she was young, but only started writing them down in the last dozen years. After publishing a couple of short stories, 'Down and Out' is her first official published novel.

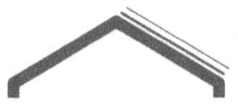

Main Cast of Undercity:

Teddy – Second oldest child of Peterson family
    Eyes – brown
  Hair – chestnut
  Complexion – Khaki
  Build – slight

Caden – Oldest child of Peterson family
  Eyes – amber
  Hair – black twists
  Complexion – sepia brown
  Build – tall, boney

Jolon – Middle child of Peterson family
  Eyes – mud brown
  Hair – curly black
  Complexion – copper
  Build – thick

Deb - youngest child of Peterson family
  Eyes – pale blue
  Hair – light blond
  Complexion – ivory
  Build – slight

  Cate – Friend of Caden
  Eye - grey-blue
  Hair – Rusty Red
  Complexion – pale
  Build –short, slender

Mr. Truman Peterson
  Eyes – pale blue
  Hair – black and grey
  Complexion – drywall grey
  Build – boney

Mrs. Tisha Peterson
  Eyes – grey
  Hair – frizzy blonde
  Complexion – drywall grey
  Build – tall

Henri – brute for Peterson family
  Eyes – forest green

Hair – thin / dusky brown
Complexion – freckled white
Build – slight

Georges – Upperlord and Brute Merchant
Eyes – gold
Hair – black and grey braids
Complexion – coal black
Build – boney

Belinda – Upperlord and Brute Merchant
Eyes – gold
Hair – black braids and twists
Complexion – coal black
Build – full-figured

Mrs. Fish – Friend of Peterson family
Eyes – gold
Hair – mahogany
Complexion – tawny
Build – tall / physically fit

Mr. Fish – Friend of Peterson family
Eyes – brown
Hair – black
Complexion – copper with beard
Build – brawn

Dorkas – Fellow Underling

Eyes – grey
Hair – grey
Complexion – grey
Build – narrow

Nuna – Tower Resident
    Eyes – brown
    Hair – chestnut
    Complexion – rusty
    Build – solid

Keme – Brute and friend of Henri's
    Eyes – grey-gold
    Hair – dark brown
    Complexion – ruddy-brown
    Build – thick, muscular

Cratchen – Underling, friend of Cate
    Eyes – green
    Hair – blond
    Complexion – pasty white
    Build – skin and bone

Jemma – Wife of Nuna

Eyes – dark gold
Hair – black
Complexion – deep brown
Build – square, solid